T0162001

NOTHING CAN RESCUE ME

NOTHING CAN RESCUE ME

Elizabeth Daly

NOTHING CAN RESCUE ME

A Felony & Mayhem mystery

PRINTING HISTORY
First U.S. hardcover edition (Farrar & Rinehart): 1943
First U.S. paperback edition (Bantam): 1946
Felony & Mayhem edition: 2008

ISBN 978-1-933397-88-7

Manufactured in the United States of America

-Contents

NOTHING CAN RESCUE ME

CHAPTER ONE

Some Silly Game

THE PLUMP LITTLE MAN LEANED OVER Gamadge's shoulder and squeaked in his ear: "Who am I?"

"Hutter!"

"It's a wonder you knew me." Sylvanus Hutter circled Gamadge's chair, pulled one up for himself, and sat down. He smiled and rubbed his knees. "That last reunion was in 1927."

"Good Heavens." Gamadge had laid aside his magazine, to gaze benevolently at his old classmate. "'27 from '42 leaves fifteen."

"That's New York for you! But of course I'm always on the wing; or was," his face fell, "until recently. Life will be different for awhile, I suppose."

"Plenty of things to see on our continent."

"I don't suppose I shall have time to see them. As for digging! Good-bye to the digs for the duration."

"Perhaps you'll have time to get out another handsome

1

book. I see them, if I don't see you." Gamadge added: "Nice of you to tap me."

"I was going to call you up. Lucky to find you at the old club."

"I shouldn't be here if my wife weren't away."

"Oh, is she? That's too bad. Florence and I hoped you'd both be able to come up to Underhill to-morrow for over Sunday. We've never met Mrs. Gamadge—too absurd."

"She's in the West; her aunt's ill there, and needed her."

"But you'll come, Gamadge, old man?"

Gamadge, as he considered the question, thought that fifteen years had not made much difference in Sylvanus Hutter. He was old for thirty-six—his lightish hair was thinning, his pinkish face had developed creases that would soon be wrinkles; but he was still as neat as a pin, and still punctilious—if he had dressed for a solitary dinner at the club; his yellow-brown eyes were still unable squarely to meet the eyes of the person he was talking to; his manner, in spite of a touch of nervousness, was as deliberate as of old. Sylvanus had never caught trains; he had advanced upon them with quiet purpose, ignoring their clamour and the rush of the crowd.

The round eyes besought Gamadge, and shifted away. "Florence will be disappointed if you can't manage the weekend—what's left of it." He added: "Dine with me and think it over."

"Awfully sorry, I'm meeting some men for bridge and dinner. Wish I were not; I'm straight from the office."

"You in an office?"

"Bit of a war job. I'd like to go up to Underhill; I haven't seen Florence for five years—since her wedding. You don't see much of people at their weddings."

"I wasn't at the wedding. Couldn't get home for it." Hutter was still rubbing his plump knees, "I was laid up abroad."

"So you were." Gamadge remembered a theory, current at

the time, that if Sylvanus had not been stranded in Rome with a broken leg his Aunt Florence would never have rushed into, and gone through with, her unsuitable marriage.

"Florence says you really must come to-morrow; I mean, you really must." Hutter's straying eyes rose from Gamadge's tie to his face, and remained there. "It's—it's a case, you know."

"A case?"

"For you. At least, Florence thinks it is. I don't as yet agree with her. I still think it may be some silly game."

"I have no time for cases, Syl; my assistant's in camp, my own job's shot to pieces, and I'm up to my ears in war work."

"Surely you could give us to-morrow and Sunday?"

"I'd have to leave on Sunday afternoon. I must be in that office by nine on Monday morning."

"You could probably clear the whole thing up overnight. We know," said Hutter, smiling, "what a great man you are."

This was a joke—a Hutter joke. Greatness, even to the present sophisticated generation of Hutters, meant an ability to make a great deal of money; except in the case of a few persons, most of whom had been dead a long time.

"Don't tease me," begged Gamadge.

"Tease you? We're only thankful we know a fellow like you. The matter's confidential, very ticklish, Florence is upset. She needs a man of sense to confer with."

"Her husband doesn't qualify?" Gamadge, remembering Tim Mason the cheerful idiot, the muscular sportsman, who had succeeded at last where other, wiser fortune hunters had failed, asked the question with raised eyebrows.

Hutter laughed, "I think you know Tim Mason!"

"I knew him once—slightly. I haven't seen him since the wedding, either."

"Well, he's sixteen years younger than Florence, and you can guess that she didn't marry him because he was sensible."

"He must be forty now."

Hutter wagged his head. "He's no help in a matter of this kind. He won't take it seriously."

"You say you don't take it seriously, whatever it is."

"Well; I—at first I didn't. Now I'm beginning to wonder whether it oughtn't to be looked into after all."

"What's it all about, anyway?"

"I'm ashamed to say that it seems to be all about spooks." Hutter laughed without much heartiness.

"I'm no authority on them, my dear boy."

"Poor Florrie thinks *she* is. She took up automatic writing, and planchette, and all the rest of it, some time ago. Sally Deedes got her into it—you remember Sally? She's been in a state of distraction for a great while, what with her marriage going to pieces, and her shop, and taxes, and the war. To tell you the truth, Gamadge, I ask myself whether Sally isn't doing the things herself; unconsciously, of course. I ask myself whether Florence isn't!"

Gamadge was irritated. "What things? What things?"

"Don't ask me; it's all above my head. I'd only confuse you and myself if I attempted to explain. You must come and get it straight from Florence, you really must."

Gamadge sat back to study Florence Mason's nephew with knitted brows. If Syl's complacence had been disturbed, something very disagreeable must be going on at Underhill. Gamadge would not have been surprised to hear that trouble had followed the Mason marriage, but he would not have expected the trouble to proceed from the spirit world.

He thought of Florence's wedding. She had carried it off well, with the childlike confidence that disarms criticism, and the cool determination that overrides it. She had looked younger than her fifty-one years, if a trifle haggard in her smart bridal gown and veil. She had been fluttery, emotional, triumphant. Mason, thick-shouldered and blond, the picture of satisfaction and good humour, had crushed the bones of Gamadge's hand.

"Isn't she a wonderful girl, old man?" And Florence had embraced Gamadge, had cried, had shown him Syl's lovely cable from Rome.

"Henry darling," she had quavered, "why don't you get married?"

Gamadge had benignly wished them luck. Now he passed the imbecile query on to Sylvanus Hutter: "Why don't you get married, Syl?"

"Me?" Hutter was almost resentful. "Why should I get married? I'm perfectly happy as I am—or was, until this wretched war stopped my work. I don't even know what will happen to my new book—the Mexican book. The fellow who was helping me with the text—clever boy—has gone off to fight."

Gamadge respected the taste, the industry, and the knowledge that went into Hutter's art-and-travel books, published at his own expense in luxurious style, and illustrated for the most part with photographs of places and objects taken by Hutter himself. And Hutter collected things, too. Gamadge asked: "Did you bring much stuff home with you?"

"Oh, no; that isn't my field, you know; my field is closed. And my collecting wasn't ever to be taken seriously, in any case; I hadn't the money to buy much of anything really good. But Florence was worried about our best things—she has some nice silver and glass, you know; she insisted on having it all crated—waterproof crating—and bringing it up to Underhill. She thinks we might bury it."

"No, really?"

"Florence wouldn't stay in New York after the air wardens began to come around. She was frightened."

"I wondered how you all happened to be in Underhill in February."

"We went up on the first, for the duration."

"Dear me! I had no idea people were evacuating themselves."

"Oh, Florence was determined to go. We closed the New York house, and we've taken a little apartment. We all run down, now and then. This is the twentieth, isn't it? We've been up at Underhill nearly three weeks."

"What on earth does Mason find to do with himself at Underhill?"

"Oh, he's quite happy. He has his horses, and he's planning a nine-hole golf course across the stream. He comes to town a good deal, runs about, follows the races. Florence keeps the house full of people, you know. We're very gay." But Sylvanus did not look gay.

"She always did love a houseful." Gamadge smiled, remembering Underhill in former days.

"Yes. She was fairly happy until this wretched business came along. Somebody's been playing tricks. Until yesterday, though, I hoped that if we paid no attention the nonsense would stop. Yesterday—to be frank with you, I was disturbed; I let Florence persuade me that we'd better call you in. Miss Wing was inclined to wait a little."

"Miss Wing?"

"Florence's secretary."

"Florence has a secretary, has she?"

"Oh, yes. She's had several. She needs somebody to do her cheques and her social correspondence, get the household bills straight, that kind of thing. As a matter of fact, I've often been glad of someone to do my own accounts when I'm busy. And Miss Wing is a very highly educated girl, and she's been indispensable," said Hutter, smiling a little, "since Florence began to write."

"Florence is writing? Splendid." Gamadge himself refrained from smiling.

"For a year or so she tried plays, but she seemed to have a good deal of trouble with them, so she decided to attempt a novel. She started it as soon as she got to Underhill, and she's been at it tooth and nail."

"Good for Florence."

"It was just what she needed to keep her busy up there. Miss Wing was invaluable—gave her her head, and did all the hard work. She's a most cultivated, accomplished girl, a cousin of Sally Deedes. Has a bachelor's degree, fell on hard times. Florence is devoted to her. She's lasted," said Hutter simply, "four years."

"It sounds as if she had plenty to do."

"She earns her salary, but you know Florence—how extremely good she is to people she likes. Miss Wing hoped at first that she'd be able to get to the bottom of this trouble we've been having—clear it up herself. But Florence and I think it's gone too far; it ought to be stopped."

"How long has it been going on?"

"A couple of weeks."

"Who's been in the house while it was going on?"

"That's the worst of it—that's why Florence is so badly upset. Eliminating the servants—and we can eliminate them, as you will see—"

"Tell me now why we can eliminate them."

"They're mentally incapable of such a trick. Besides—ridiculous! You remember dear old Thomas, and Florence's Louise; devotion itself. The others—well, they're out of the question. When you hear the story you'll know what I mean."

"I hope so."

"Just take my word for it that the thing needed brains, brains and a debased kind of imagination. You know, Gamadge, that I have very little imagination myself; I take things coolly, I don't go off the handle. But this business has given me a very queer feeling; unless Florence or Sally has quite gone off her head, hang it all, there's something ugly in the house. Bad feeling, I mean."

"Who was there besides the servants, Syl?" asked Gamadge patiently.

"Mason and myself, Sally Deedes, Miss Wing, Susie Burt, and a young fellow named Percy. Did you ever know Susie Burt? She would have been a child when you used to stay at Underhill."

"I remember a beautiful Mrs. Burt."

"That was Susie's mother, Florence's best friend. She died, her husband died, and Susie's their only child. Susie's had practically no income for some years. Florence took her on, tried to make her into a secretary just before she married Mason. It didn't work; Susie's not up to it. She stays with us a good deal—awfully pretty, very good company when she wants to be—and she has had various jobs from time to time here in town. None of them was very solid or lasting. Florence thinks she's forward with men, but of course the poor girl wants be married. I never saw any great harm in her myself."

"Who's Percy?"

"He's an old friend of Susie's, charming fellow, been coming to Underhill with the Burts since he was a child. Great favourite with Florence; has no people, writes or something, lots of personality. Mason thinks he's affected, but it's only his way. He's from Georgia originally, but he now lives in New York."

"Do all these people know about the unpleasantness, whatever it is?"

"Oh, yes. Florence talked of nothing else. Now she's talking about nothing else but you."

"You say it may be some silly game. Miss Wing more or less agrees?"

Sylvanus, rather uncomfortably, said she did.

"How do the others react?"

"Mason declares it's a stupid joke, meant to tease Florence; that's more or less what I think and Miss Wing thinks, but he's amused and we're not; his sensibilities aren't too fine, you know. Susie Burt has no opinion—her mind's a blank on the subject. Percy won't express himself at all—but then he's out of it—no axe to grind. I mean—" Hutter coughed. "He's too intelligent to do such a thing, if you know what I mean; just as Susie isn't intelligent enough."

"I don't in the least know what you mean; you won't tell me."

"He's too intelligent. Wouldn't bother. Sally says it's the spirits."

"Says the spirits are playing a trick on Florence?"

"She's really not herself since her divorce from Bill."

"And you occasionally wonder whether she or Florence isn't playing the trick in some trance?"

"Only because any other theory seems so incredible. Florence is badly upset, Gamadge." He looked suddenly piteous.

"I'll come if she needs me."

"Needs you? She begs you to come. She implores you to come."

Gamadge's mind travelled back through the years; to school and college vacations when his mother and father had been far away, and he had been invited to Underhill. He remembered the glorious food, the parties, the winter sports, the camping and fishing, the pretty girls. He remembered Miss Florence Hutter presiding over the household and spoiling Syl's friends; lively, affectionate, kind, but subject to sudden tempers and jealousies, easily bored with her protégés, easily made suspicious of their loyalty. Domineering—too domineering to marry while she was young. She had always seemed to Gamadge extraordinarily vulnerable in spite of her shrewdness.

"Well, I shan't be able to stay long enough to do much good," he said. "As I told you, I must go back on Sunday."

Hutter, expelling a long breath, seemed also to expel care. He instantly got to his feet, gently shook one leg and then the other, and spoke with all his normal serenity: "Thank goodness. Mason and I are driving up to-night in his two-seater, but the big car's in town being overhauled, and I'll have Smith pick you up to-morrow morning. Will nine be too early? It will get you up to Underhill in time for a talk with Florence before lunch."

"I'll be ready."

"And I'll telephone Florence now. Take a load off her mind." Sylvanus hesitated, and assumed the look that Hutters assumed when they were about to discuss money. "By the way, Florence expects you to accept a fee."

"Very nice of her."

"People sting her awfully, but she knows you won't. We don't know the proper fee for consultation, but Florence thought she might suggest what she pays her specialist for a visit—a hundred."

"Well, I don't know," said Gamadge, enjoying himself. "Let's say no remuneration unless I exorcise the spirits from Underhill; and if I do, she can pay me what she pays Macloud—if he's still her lawyer—for exorcising some of the decimals out of her supertax."

"Oh, good God, my dear fellow!" Hutter looked frightened.

"That or nothing," smiled Gamadge.

"Talk it over with Florence; and Smith shall drive you home on Sunday."

Sylvanus shook hands warmly, and trotted off. Gamadge mounted to a vast brown room, on an upper floor, and sought a lean man who was reading in a corner. "Hi," he said.

"Hi."

"Nobody here—we can talk."

"No, we can't. I'm busy."

"I want to know how Nahum Hutter left his money, and how much he left."

Mr. Robert Macloud raised his saturnine visage from the *Law Journal*, but maintained a grip on it. He said: "Nahum left about ten millions. Florence and Sylvanus have the use of the income, share and share alike, until one of them dies. The survivor—presumably Syl—then gets the whole capital, and can spend it."

"You don't say." Gamadge let himself down into the depths of a leather chair.

"Nahum fixed it that way for his two children, Florence and Washington; Washington and Mrs. Washington died, and Nahum transferred the arrangement to Florence and Syl—Washington's only child."

"What income do Florence and Syl struggle along on?"

"About a hundred thousand apiece, taxes paid; that's what they have now."

"No provision for heirs, if any?"

"None. Old Ben Hutter didn't make his fortune from railroads until Nahum was grown. Nahum was born and brought up in something like poverty on the original Hutter farm. He seems to have made up his mind that Florence and Syl should be comfortable as long as they lived; I suppose he thought that the survivor would have so much money he or she simply couldn't lose it." He added after reflection: "And I suppose he thought Florence wouldn't marry—she was forty when he died, and had turned all fortune hunters down. Very funny; there must be something about Mason that I missed."

"I faintly remember Nahum as quite a terror."

"A pet, compared to old Ben. Nahum was rather proud of his children; he liked their social success; but Ben Hutter cast his other son, Joel, into outer darkness because he wanted to stay home and fish in the stream. They had a frightful row; Ben didn't leave him a cent."

"Did he mind?"

"Don't know; but he died."

"Would it be indiscreet of me to ask if Florence and Syl have made wills?"

"You mean you want to know what's in 'em. No secret about Syl's; he hasn't much to leave. So far he's lived well up to his income, you know how—travel, financing excavations, putting out his books. What he has goes to museums."

"Queer situation, in a way; both of 'em as rich as Solomon, and neither can make an impressive will until the other dies."

"You're quite wrong; Florence can make a very good will indeed. *She* never financed digs; in the good old days she took her savings and went on the market. Just like her father, has the Midas touch. She made half a million."

"Be a good scout and tell me how she's leaving it."

"What are you, that you should be told?"

"It wouldn't be ethical of me to say."

"You have no monopoly on ethics. And even if I did tell you, the information might cease to be of value any day. Florence, I am sorry to say it, has become a will-shaker."

"Has she, though?"

"You been seeing them of late years?"

"Not for fifteen, except that glimpse I had of her at her wedding."

"That wedding was her Rubicon."

"She seemed pretty much then as she had always been, except that her poor face had been lifted."

"She's turned despot, and is surrounded by slaves. Even Syl, who's financially independent of her, must do as he's told, or he'd have to go—the house wouldn't hold him."

"Mason?"

"I'm not quite sure how much influence Mason still has, and I shall have no further opportunities for observation. They've fired me."

"Syl and Florence have? What on earth for?"

Macloud made a face. "For sending in a bill, I suppose. They have a failing which they share with some other rich persons—they think paupers ought to work for them for love."

"I'm going up there to-morrow on a job."

Macloud removed his cigar to glance alertly at his friend. "Job? Books? Papers? Autographs? Didn't know Syl bothered with them."

"He didn't really say what the job was."

"Nothing in the criminological line, I presume? Ah, well;

get the amount of your honorarium down in writing first, my boy, and take my blessing with you."

"I m doing whatever it is on spec."

"Heaven help you."

Gamadge, frowning, lighted a cigarette. "Florence was awfully good to me when I was young," he said. "My father had to travel for his health, and my mother naturally went along; the Hutters took me in for holidays. Florence was awfully kind."

"She's still kind; sometimes too kind. Then she gets tired of people, or suspicious of them, or something, and it's all off. The set-up there isn't too healthy, I sometimes think."

"That's what I thought, from what Sylvanus told me tonight."

"Well, I'm out of the picture now, thank goodness. Go away and leave me in peace, why don't you?"

Gamadge went away, but only to the opposite corner of the room. He got some books out of a glassed case, and settled down to read everything he could find on automatic writing, with special reference to the use of planchette.

But his thoughts would wander to Underhill in the old days; he remembered sitting in the Gothic dining-room at meal-times and wondering, as he listened to the homilies of Nahum Hutter, that Florence and Sylvanus were as decent as they were; for Nahum's homilies were variations upon one theme—that we live, after all, by our pockets, and that the man or woman who has something to give away must never hope to possess entirely disinterested friends.

CHAPTER TWO

Chapter Nine

AFTER CROSSING THE HUDSON AT POUGHKEEPSIE the big Hutter car travelled north-west. It followed an excellent highway through the town of Bethea, and then bore off to the left and rolled sixteen miles into mountain country. Beyond the village of Erasmus (fourteen houses, a store, a church, and a handsome library) it turned left again, to proceed with due caution along a dirt road harrowed by winter storms. Gamadge looked out at the landscape that he had once known so well; at the hillsides covered with immemorial hemlock, the later growths of beech and maple in the valleys, the rocky fields and brown streams. Strange, wild country; haunted country in the past, when no Indian would camp where the hemlocks made day into night. Haunted country still, legend declared, on the mountains.

Three miles above Erasmus the Hutter house stood on its ridge, with a view to the south-west of Catskill ranges. It was sheltered on the east by a towering slope of hemlock, the hill that had given it its present name; a stream ran below the grounds to the west, and beyond it were cultivated fields and pastures. Long ago Underhill had been the Hutter Farm, but old Ben Hutter had come back to it in triumph after he made his fortune, and rebuilt it of field stone into a fine large house, a typical summer residence of the 'eighties. It was a kind of villa, like the villas that old Hutter was now invited to outside New York; he admired them very much, and saw no reason why one of them should not be set down among the hemlock forests. It was weather-tight, three stories high, and almost square, with a lawn and a carriage house. It had a bathroom, but water did not run in the house. It had no plumbing. Large fires burned on its hearths on all but a few summer evenings, and it was lighted by kerosene. It was not meant to be lived in during cold weather.

At the turn of the century when old Hutter died, his son Nahum allowed his children to modernize the house. They christened it Underhill, and introduced another bathroom, hot and cold running water, and sanitation. The grounds were land-scaped, and there was a library.

By the time Nahum died—in 1925—Underhill made its own electricity, had an oil burner in the cellar and lost slices from its bedrooms; the slices became individual baths. Florence and Sylvanus came up at all seasons of the year, and steadily refused to do anything about the three miles of bad road from Erasmus; they were only too glad to be cut off from the tourist traffic.

By February 1942, when Gamadge stepped out of the car and looked at Underhill, it had encountered decorative art. The field stone had been filled in with stucco, and washed a delicate pink; a tracery of ironwork surrounded its roof and climbed up its walls; its pointed windows were now arches, and its porch had been shaved away. Gamadge stood upon shallow front steps and gazed at it. He feared for the once stately interior, but he ought to have trusted Florence and Syl and their decorator; when he had greeted old Thomas affectionately and entered the hall he was delighted. Underhill's dignity had been preserved, but its grimness was gone.

"Well, Thomas," he said, "I'm glad to be walking on the old black-and-white marble again, and I must say it looks better than it ever did before."

"Yes, sir. All the white does brighten up the house. But it's a dark house, sir."

"So it is. These high, narrow windows."

"Mrs. Mason would like to see you upstairs, sir. It's very nice to have you with us again."

"Very nice to be here."

Sylvanus popped from the library on the left. "Gamadge—this is splendid. Florence wants to see you, but will you have something to warm you up first? You must have had a cold journey."

"Warm as toast. Not a thing, thank you, Syl."

"I've put you in your old room, the one next to mine. Hope you don't mind sharing my bath?"

"Of course not."

"I'll see you when you come down."

Gamadge was glad that a stalwart Scandinavian maid possessed herself of his bag. He followed the ancient Thomas up to the second floor and along its wide corridor to the back of the house. Thomas knocked at an end door, opened it, and stood aside.

Underhill might be a dark house, but Florence Mason had contrived a bright room for herself by having partitions removed and securing an outlook to the north, south and west. She sat beside the crackling fire in what seemed a flood of sunlight, although the February sun was pale; sat among her light-blue draperies, on a tufted chaise-longue, and held out her arms to him.

"Henry, darling Henry, I'm so glad you could come!"

Gamadge went over and hugged her. "Of course I came."

"You haven't changed a bit" She kept both his hands in a nervous grip when he straightened to look down at her. He couldn't say the same; she had changed a good deal. Whatever her maid Louise could do had been done for her, but Florence herself had ceased to take an interest in herself. Her hair, dyed a bright brown, had not been carefully rearranged for him as it would have been in earlier days, and she had painted a purplish-red mouth crookedly over her own. She had aged greatly since her marriage; her round hazel eyes had lost all their brightness. She looked as though she no longer cared to be young, and had no idea how to be old.

"Dear Florrie," said Gamadge.

Her ringed hands jerked at his. "I was so frightfully disappointed when Syl told me your wife was away, Henry. Why did you marry her in Arizona or somewhere? I've never laid eyes on the child."

"I'll bring her up to see you when she gets home." He looked about him, pulled up a satinwood chair, and sat down. "I'm not at all sure that I like the idea of your staying up here indefinitely. You'll be bored, and that's not good for you or anybody."

"We often go to town. I got so upset with the blackouts and everything that I couldn't stay in New York. Even if we blackout here, it won't seem so *close* to the war. I feel so safe here. I mean I did feel so safe, till these things happened. At first I was just angry."

"And aren't you now?"

"No. I'm frightened. Henry—" she clutched at his hand again—"Henry—I'm not doing the things myself. I'm not crazy."

"Definitely you're not."

"Tell them so! Tell everybody I'm not doing the things myself!"

"You must first tell me all about it, Florrie; that's what I'm here for."

She sat back against her blue-satin pillows. "I know you won't laugh and say it's a joke. That's what Tim says."

"Perhaps he's just trying to reassure you. Tell me about it."

"Well, you see, I began to write a novel. I can hardly bear to think of it now."

"Oh, why? It seemed to me so sporting of you."

Mrs. Mason's face brightened a little. "I liked doing it, Henry. I was never so surprised in my life—it wasn't hard at all!"

"What a clever girl you are."

"I know they say there's a story in everyone's life, if we could only write it."

"If."

"And of course the story in my life was Tim and me. Our affair. I thought I'd write it, making myself of course very much younger. So that it would be more popular, you know." She looked at him anxiously.

"One makes these concessions to the tastes of the larger public."

"Our affair, Tim's and mine, was so interesting and so unusual. Of course the romance doesn't last."

"Doesn't it?"

"They say not. But when I began to write, it all came back to me. The ideas seemed actually to flow!"

"Did they?" Gamadge's eye wandered rather apprehensively to a sheaf of manuscript on a table at Mrs. Mason's elbow.

"I dictate to my secretary, Evelyn Wing. Then she types out what we've done, and next day we discuss it. If it needs revising, she types it again."

"What I call an ideal arrangement."

"I have no trouble at all. Evelyn looks up things for me, and makes such excellent suggestions. She's very highly educated, you know, so I don't have to worry about making mistakes."

"You seem to have a paragon there."

"Oh, I couldn't live without her now! It's not only that she's clever; she's so good to me. So kind. I regard her as one of my best and dearest friends." Mrs. Mason looked at him with what seemed a touch of bravado.

"Why not?"

"She runs the household, she does our cheque-books and answers invitations, and when I had flu last year she sat up all night until Dr. Burbage sent a nurse. She isn't silly about men, and she doesn't fly into a temper if I get nervous."

"You're not getting too dependent on her, Florrie? These young people move on; they have their own lives to lead."

"Evelyn won't leave me while I need her. You know—I get cross, sometimes, Henry." She gave him a sidelong look. "People are so provoking."

"They are."

"Instead of taking offence she just sits quietly and waits for me to get over it. Even Sally Deedes takes offence sometimes, when I rage to her about Bill."

"Sally found this treasure for you?"

"Yes, Sally's her cousin—much older, of course. Evelyn's people all died, and she had no money, and she went through a dreadful time. Sally told me; Evelyn never talks about it."

Gamadge silently agreed that Miss Wing must have had a dreadful time.

"I've made Father's den into an office for her. You remember the den?"

Gamadge remembered it, and the rather wolfish old gentleman who had growled in it.

"Evelyn typed my novel in the den every night. Then she took the page she had got to out of the typewriter and left it on top of the pile of script." Mrs. Mason turned to pick up the clipped sheaf of papers from the little stand beside her. "We were on Chapter Nine; here's all we've done of it." She handed him the sheets, and suddenly there was stark tenor in her eyes. "Please look at Page 83."

Gamadge looked at *her*, and then turned to Page 83. "Now begin at the marked paragraph."

Gamadge found the marked paragraph, and read aloud:

Gloria buried her yellow curls in the cushion, and beat her small clenched fist against the back of the sofa. Sobs shook her slender body. Roy was beside her in two strides. He crushed her in his arms.

"Go away," she choked.

Roy held her closer. "I won't go," he said huskily, "until you listen to me."

LISTEN TO *ME*, SAID THE DEMON, AS HE PLACED HIS HAND UPON MY HEAD.

Gamadge stared, looked up at Mrs. Mason, and stared again. "What on earth?" he at last demanded.

Mrs. Mason's lips were pressed tightly together.

"Somebody wrote that in?" he asked.

"There it was, all in big capitals, when Evelyn went and got the script the next morning. A week ago yesterday."

"Friday, the thirteenth?"

"Friday, the thirteenth."

"That was overdoing it."

"I never noticed the date at the time, I was so annoyed. It seemed like such a silly kind of joke, and nobody would own up to it. And it sounded so *wicked*, somehow. Not like a joke at all. I don't see how anybody thought of it. It's too senseless. It's too *strange*."

"Poe is considered rather strange at times," said Gamadge.

"Poe!"

"Yes. E. A. Poe. It's a quotation from Poe."

"Well, I must say I'm glad to hear it; it makes everything a little less uncanny, even the other ones."

"Are there other ones?"

"Wait until you see them. This is nothing."

"And you say nobody in the house realized that it was a quotation from anybody?"

"No. Ought they to have recognized it? Of course I shouldn't."

"I don't think the average person would recognize it; I do, because I just happen to know the piece it comes from: 'Silence—A Fable.' It's a good deal more sinister in this context than it is in its own. Miss Wing seems to have gone on from it as if it were part of the text."

"She wanted to throw the page away and say nothing about it; she was annoyed, because it seemed to be poking fun at me, in a way; at my book."

"Queer way to go at it."

"Too queer. I wouldn't let her touch it! I wanted to leave it right in the page, just as it was. We found it that Friday, as I said, and on Saturday morning we found—look at Page 89."

She watched him as he did so. He read the marked passage:

> Gloria told herself again and again that she would never get over it. She whispered to herself that she would be unhappy always. And she had been so carefree, so happy and busy, until Roy came into her life.

YOU SHALL FULLY KNOW
THAT YOUR ESTATE
IS OF THE TWO THE FAR MORE DESPERATE.

Gamadge communed with this for a moment in silence. Then he looked up at Mrs. Mason. "Surely," he said, "you all realized that this is a quotation."

"No, we didn't."

"Syl didn't? Miss Wing didn't?"

"Nobody did. We just thought it was queer—like the other."

"It isn't queer like the other. It's from George Herbert; it's from a poem called 'A Paradox.' Lovely thing."

"I never heard of it, and I don't remember ever having heard of George Herbert, either."

"Did you still think that somebody was playing a peculiar joke on you?"

"I was sure they were making fun of my novel. I made an awful fuss. Is it so funny?" asked Mrs. Mason, with a wistful look at him. "It seems to me to be just like what I read."

"It's not the kind of thing that's exactly in my line, but I should say you were making a very good job of it. What does Miss Wing say about your work?"

"She won't criticize anything but the grammar and punctuation and that sort of thing. She says she never can get any perspective on the work of people she knows."

"She seems to be a person of great intelligence indeed." Gamadge looked down at Page 89, and said: "I see that you and she went sternly on, in spite of these curious additions to the text."

"We certainly did go on. I told everybody that if the jokes went on I should find out who was doing it, and I'd never forgive them. It would be the end. Now Page 92—we hadn't the heart to do more than three pages on Saturday. See what we found on Sunday morning."

Gamadge read:

Gloria laughed until the tears came. Roy begged: "Don't laugh at me, sweetheart! I can stand anything else, but please don't laugh!"

"But you're so funny, Roy! A great big man like you on his knees!"

LADY! LAUGH, BE MERRY; TIME IS PRECIOUS.

When Gamadge looked up from this, his face was grave. Mrs. Mason said quickly: "That's the way Evelyn looked when she saw it."

"She noticed a change of tone?"

"It—it seems to *warn* me."

"There is an implied threat. Here—keep calm, Florrie; don't go off the handle, now; I need your co-operation."

Mrs. Mason tore at her handkerchief. "We decided to sit up and watch, at least Evelyn did. Nothing happened, of course; it's impossible to do anything in this house without everybody else knowing about it. I couldn't work on Sunday or Monday, but I did a few pages on Tuesday, and I absolutely forced myself to do some more on Wednesday! I had to know what was coming! But on Thursday morning I couldn't stand it; I made Syl get hold of you."

On the last page but one Gamadge read:

"Oh, it's such fun just to be alive!" Gloria threw herself into Roy's arms, and buried her face on his shoulder.
"I'm glad we're both alive," he murmured into her
ear.

THOU ART BUT DEAD; IF THOU HAVE ANY GRACE, PRAY.

Mrs. Mason, anxiously waiting until he had finished, burst out in a wail: "What is it from, Henry? What is it from?"

"Play by John Ford; and so's the other—unless I'm much mistaken." Gamadge lifted angry eyes to hers. "Keep calm, Florrie. They may very well just be tasteless fooling with your text."

"Look at the last one." Mrs. Mason's tone was the quiet tone of one who is reconciled to the worst. "Look at the last one, and then say it's tasteless fooling!"

"Now, don t forget that they're all quotations; I should have thought anybody would know that, just to glance at them."

"I didn't know it; and that lets me out, Henry; and besides, I can't even type!"

Gamadge turned to the last page. He read Mrs. Mason's harmless lines, and then the great and terrible words that followed them:

> "But I'm so lonely, Roy, in this great big house." Gloria clung to him, "People think I have everything, but I'm so lonely!"
>
> "Just you give me a ring, day or night, and I'll come, he promised tenderly. "I don't care if it's three in the morning, I'll come, and you can talk to me out of the window."
>
> "Oh, it's wonderful to know that you're there!"

WHATSOEVER NOISE YE HEAR, COME NOT UNTO ME, FOR NOTHING CAN RESCUE ME.

Gamadge, rearranging the pages of Chapter Nine, said in a voice of cold disgust: "Marlowe; *Doctor Faustus*."

CHAPTER THREE

Being of Sound Mind

A GLIMMER OF SATISFACTION could be observed in Mrs. Mason's eye; she had sampled her Compendium of Useful Knowledge, was sure that it contained the answers to all her problems, and now prepared to buy it: "Henry, you know everything. I'll give you five thousand dollars if you'll find out who put those quotations into my book, and why they did it."

"Fair enough." Gamadge laid Chapter Nine on his knees, gave Mrs. Mason a cigarette, and lighted it and his own. "But I never may find out, you know. Crime in the family circle—it often goes unpunished, you know. I'm certain of one thing, Florrie; you didn't do it. All these authors didn't lie buried in your unconscious."

"Do you think automatic writing is just what is in your mind all the time?" She asked it wistfully.

"I do. Many people disagree with me."

"Sally Deedes is sure it's spirits; but she's psychic, and I'm not."

Gamadge frowned. "What has transformed that once sceptical and frivolous creature? She used to be as materialistic as anybody I ever knew in my life."

"She's had so much trouble, Henry; with Bill, you know. I managed to make her divorce him at last, but she's still broken-hearted. After a year! The occult takes her mind off him."

"Let her take the medicine that agrees with her, but let her not hand it on to you. That medicine doesn't agree with everybody." He added, removing his cigarette to look at her sharply: "*You* don't think the spirits annotated your script, do you?"

"Sometimes I hardly know what to think; I'd rather think that than think other things! Since Thursday—" she cast a glance at her bewitched novel, and looked away from it again—"I have been dreadfully nervous at night. These doors are all so thick, and they fit so tight; I don't believe anybody would hear me if I did—make a noise."

'Don't let this joker undermine your morale. The thing was meant to scare you, you know; let's give our anthologist a bit of a disappointment. Why are you so marooned at night? Have you no bell?"

"No, I've never needed Louise in the night-time. I'm only too glad to get rid of her. You know what she's like— practically on top of me all day."

"Er—what about Mason?"

"Tim has his own room—that little one that used to be Father's dressing-room, beyond the bath."

Gamadge looked over his shoulder at a closed door in the east wall. "Why don't you and he keep the communicating doors open?"

"He likes them shut."

"Let him forget what he likes," said Gamadge indignantly. "I never heard such stuff."

"It's on my account," explained Mrs. Mason. "He doesn't like to disturb me. He gets up early, and sometimes he comes in late."

"Tell him you wish to be disturbed, at least until you get to the bottom of this foolery. It's a damned shame that you should be left alone at night to scare yourself into fits."

"I won't ask favours of him." She seemed likely to burst into tears. "I have some pride left."

Gamadge, rather perturbed, considered her in silence. He said at last: "I'll have a word with Mason."

"No, Henry; I forbid you!" Her round eyes gleamed at him through tears. "I absolutely forbid you."

"Well, I'm not sure that I don't think you're right. Much better to have Louise in with you than one of the suspects." He patted her arm as she began to sob. "Now, please, Florrie! If we're to investigate; we must do it properly. If you want to find out who played this horrid game with you, you must go right at it like a policeman; leave no loopholes. That's the only way. Have Louise in with you at night."

She dried her eyes. "All right, I will. I'm sorry, but it's all so miserable. I've done so much for them all. I give Sally her clothes—not my old ones, you know; I dress her. Susie Burt comes here whenever she likes, and I make her a little allowance for her rent in New York—fifty dollars a month. I settled a hundred thousand on Timothy when we married."

"He's probably spent that long ago. You can't play polo and fly aeroplanes and travel de luxe for nothing."

"Tim's given up lots of things. He's getting very economical."

"Who's paying for that private golf course?"

"It's just in case we have to give up using the cars, Henry!" She added, as he smiled at her, "People must have a little fun."

"You're mighty good to him, and I dare say to them all."

"They don't know how good!" She looked suddenly like the more formidable Florence of the old days.

"They don't know, but they may guess." He studied her for a moment, and then said briskly: "Now let's tackle this curious problem you've given me." He crossed his knees, and turned the pages of Chapter Nine. "Who in the house does a neat job of typing, and also has a more than nodding acquaintance with literature?"

Her face clouded. "That's *it*. Nobody here types as well as Evelyn, and she knows more about books than any of them, even Glen Percy."

"So far as you know. I must go into the matter myself, of course. Now as to why the thing was done. Malice, as your husband seems to insist? For if it's a joke it's a malicious one, and in fact it takes us into the field of morbid psychology; I mean that no balanced person runs the risk of losing favours present and to come by gratifying petty spite. I'm inclined to reject the theory of petty spite, anyway. It would merely have tried to make your book sound funny—much funnier than these quotations do. They're not funny at all. They're ominous."

"They were meant to frighten me."

"And that means hatred."

"If anybody hated me," said Mrs. Mason, her lip quivering, "I should know it."

"People often don't know it; tragedy is full of people who didn't know it. Assume that you're right, though, and that nobody in your house deeply hates you; there must have been some reason for playing this game, and a good reason too. Was some other effect upon you intended? Was some other effect achieved?" As she was silent, he went on: "Did anybody suggest that a special person had the means and the ability to play the trick? Suggest, in fact, that Miss Evelyn Wing had been tampering with her own typescript?"

Mrs. Mason, looking very angry, tossed her head.

"Mason insisted that it was a practical joke, meant to humiliate you. Did *he* say it must have been done by Miss Wing?"

"I knew Evelyn Wing wouldn't do a thing like that—especially if it pointed right to herself!"

"But did you know it immediately? Were you shaken at first? Do be frank with me, Florrie."

"Just at first I didn't know what to think."

"And then you had the subtle notion that it all pointed too directly to her to have been done by herself. Did *you* have the notion?" He looked her at sceptically. "Do you trust her absolutely, Florence?"

She hesitated, and then said sombrely: "There's only one person I know that I can trust absolutely; but I trust Evelyn Wing better than to—"

"Who is the person that told you Evelyn Wing couldn't have done it?"

Mrs. Mason, rather flushed, said nothing.

"Well: at least we have a point or two for the record. Mason suggested that the trick had been played by Miss Wing, out of malice."

"I'll never forgive him!"

"Mason, therefore, presumably wants to get rid of her."

"It was so small of him!"

"We have been told that a favourite has no friends. Our second point is that some person—not Miss Wing—argued you out of the idea by showing you—what? That if Miss Wing were the guilty party she would have botched the job, misspelled words, interpolated something less literary? Convinced you, in fact, that the whole thing was a plot to eliminate your secretary."

"I believe it was!"

"And what did you do about it? Or haven't you done anything yet?"

"I did do something, I can tell you! I made a new will."

"Did you indeed?" Gamadge allowed a match to go out on its way to his cigarette.

"Yes, I did. But it's temporary—until we find out who put the things in my book."

"Well, Florrie, you've been a trifle precipitate."

"This last thing was the last straw. Henry! You don't know what I've had to put up with from people. I've been meaning to make a new will for ever so long."

"When did you make the new one?"

"On Thursday afternoon."

"Quick work!"

"I'd had time to see that last awful quotation, and hear what Tim had to say, and realize that it wasn't true. I had to do something. I should have burst if I hadn't made that will."

"Did Bob Macloud draw this new will up for you?"

"No, he fussed so over the telephone that I just told him he needn't do anything for us ever again, and that I was through. When I think of the bills he sent in!"

"Bob's very discreet, Florrie," said Gamadge, smiling.

"You can carry that kind of thing too far. I told him to destroy my other will, and I just drew up the new one myself. I know exactly how, and I got the telephone man and his assistant to witness it for me. They're very nice boys, local boys; I've known them since they used to bring berries around."

"You know how to make wills, Florrie?"

"Yes, I do. I've had plenty of practice."

"I suppose you made one after you were married."

"Yes, I did. I left everything to Tim, and Bob Macloud fussed me and fussed me until I made another, a much more sensible one, about three years ago."

"Poor Bob."

"I'm quite willing to admit that it was more sensible. You know I haven't much to leave, Henry; only about five hundred thousand dollars. You know how our money's tied up?"

"You and Syl have the income."

"Until one of us dies, and of course I shall die first. So I'll never have more to leave than this five hundred thousand, which—as I keep reminding Bob—is absolutely my own to do as I like with. I earned it myself!"

"Playing the market?" Gamadge smiled at her.

"Yes, and it was hard work, I can tell you! I read the financial pages every day, and I spent hours at my broker's, sitting in front of one of those blackboards, with a lot of men."

"I bet you had a glorious time."

"It was glorious to make the money, and have something to put in a will. I never can save much out of my income now, and I don't suppose that I'll ever be able to earn much that way again. Do you?"

Gamadge said he feared not.

"Well, as I say, I felt that this five hundred thousand was my own; so about three years ago, when I made my new will, I did just as I chose in it. I left nice legacies to the servants, and annuities to Thomas and Louise, and a hundred thousand to my church in New York—dear Dr. Stokes-Burgess, I hope he'll be alive then to distribute it. He's quite a young man. It's the Church of SS. Gervase and Protase. And I left a hundred thousand to the Bethea Home for Destitute Children; Mother founded it, and I've always been interested in it. I wish I had enough to rebuild it entirely—it's dreadfully out of date, no laboratory. That left about two hundred and sixty thousand. I left twenty-five thousand apiece to Sally Deedes, Susie Burt, and Evelyn Wing. Tim was my residuary legatee; that meant a hundred and eighty-five thousand, more or less, my personal goods and chattels, and Underhill."

"Underhill is yours, is it?"

"Oh, yes; didn't you know? It costs me a fortune, too, and Syl won't do anything, though he treats it as if it belonged to him too."

"You brought him up to treat it that way."

"Well, he ought to help me with the taxes and upkeep. My

personal chattels don't amount to much—I never bought myself jewellery."

"Didn't your father buy you jewellery?"

"Just a few things. He hated buying jewellery. He thought it was a poor investment, and I suppose I caught the idea from him. Well, Bob Macloud didn't make any fuss about the will I made three years ago."

"It's not a bad will. But if Miss Wing knows what's in it, I'm not surprised that she keeps her temper when you lose yours."

"She doesn't know anything about her legacy. Nobody knows about my wills. The only will they know anything about is that first one I made after I married; I told everybody I was leaving everything to Tim. Five hundred thousand didn't seem much for him—then."

"No; I understand that."

"But Bob Macloud fussed me about Susie Burt and Sally. I think it was very good of me to leave them as much as I left Evelyn. Susie didn't keep her temper when she was my secretary; I can tell you; and I told Sally frankly that I shouldn't leave her anything if I thought she would spend it all on Bill Deedes."

Gamadge, remembering Bill Deedes's sweetness and fatal charm, groaned faintly. He murmured: "Poor Sally."

"When she promised to divorce him, I put her down for twenty-five thousand, as I said. She doesn't know how much she's getting, though. And she doesn't know that when she finally did divorce Bill, I made up my mind to leave her fifty thousand."

"Good."

"So on Thursday, when I made my new will, I gave her fifty thousand, and I gave Susie fifty thousand. And," said Mrs. Mason, looking at him defiantly, "I gave Tim fifty thousand, and I made Evelyn Wing my residuary legatee."

Gamadge sat back and stared at her. Then he said with restraint:

"Let me get this straight. The legacies to the servants, the church, and the Home, stand; Miss Burt, Sally Deedes, and your husband receive fifty thousand apiece; and your secretary gets—how much exactly?"

"It comes to about a hundred and ten thousand, I think, it and Underhill, and my personal belongings. Jewellery and stuff."

"How much does the jewellery and stuff add up to?" Gamadge glanced around the delicately furnished room.

"My furs and silver and glass and china, and the furniture and things, and my poor little brooches and bracelets and rings are appraised at fifty thousand."

"Low estimate, I think. Why Underhill to Miss Wing? Why not to Sylvanus?"

"He can buy it from Evelyn, if he wants it. He'll be rich enough to buy anything, when I die; don't forget that!"

"I'm not forgetting. Mason will fight, Florence."

"They say it's very hard to break a will." She added, rather pleadingly: "He never came back from Palm Beach when I had flu last winter; we came up here for Christmas, Syl and I, and had a party. And I couldn't get a nurse for two nights, and Evelyn sat up with me. It was so *small* of Tim to try to get rid of Evelyn!"

"Some people might not wonder at his trying to get rid of her. So you think he was the one that cooked up that business with the quotations."

"Oh, Henry, I wish I didn't think so!"

"Well, my poor, dear girl, I'm awfully sorry."

"Of course if you find out he didn't, I'll make another will."

Gamadge smiled. "This one is just to shake at Mason if I don't clear him?"

"He doesn't know anything about it yet, but he knows I don't believe Evelyn put the things in my book."

"And you telephoned Bob Macloud, and dictated this will to him on Thursday, and he cut up rough?"

"He was perfectly wild. Of course he doesn't know my reasons; he doesn't know about the things in the book, or what Evelyn means to me."

"Or that Mason didn't come back from Palm Beach when you had flu."

"Or—or anything," said Mrs. Mason, turning her head away. She looked at Gamadge again to add sharply: "It's all none of Bob's business. His business was to follow my instructions."

Gamadge rose, folded the few pages of Chapter Nine lengthwise, and put them in his pocket. He said: "I'll see all these people. I'll hold a conference after lunch from which you will be rigorously excluded. Then I'll report to you. I suppose you don't know whether the authors quoted in your script are available here—in the library?"

"No, I don't."

"And nobody, not even Syl, admits knowing that the extracts are quotations?"

"No."

"And Sally blames the spirits."

"She says a mischievous spirit sometimes gets through. She says it's a slight risk we run."

"This was a mischievous spirit indeed."

"She says it can't harm me, and that if we pay no attention to it it will go away. Like a child, you know."

"She is optimistic. You can discard that theory Florence; discard it for ever. Poe, John Ford, and Christopher Marlowe may have turned into troublesome ghosts, and they may have entered into a conspiracy to confuse and annoy authors of light fiction; I wouldn't put it past them; but count George Herbert out of it. He wouldn't spend eternity like that—he wouldn't dream of it."

Mrs. Mason gave him a watery smile. "Oh, Henry, I'm so glad you're here. You're not very spiritual, you know, but you can make me laugh."

"Oblige me by laughing, then."

She had begun to laugh, rather hysterically, when Timothy Mason emerged from the communicating bathroom. He was in his shirt sleeves. Two small griffons pranced behind him; at sight of Gamadge they exploded in a shrill chorus of barking.

CHAPTER FOUR

Mouse in the Attic

MASON HAD BEEN WORKING on his thick, light hair with a military brush. As he crossed the room he transferred the brush to his left hand, and flung out the right in a buoyant gesture of welcome.

"Hello, there, Gamadge!" He almost shouted it. "Glad to see you. You're evidently the doctor my wife needed."

Gamadge rose, smiled, and held out his own hand; but he stayed where he was. He had no sympathy with the race of griffons—it usually bit him. He allowed his fingers to be crushed again in Mason's iron paw. "Hope I'll be of use here," he said.

"You've cheered Florence up—that's all I ask. Excuse my appearance; I'm changing—had a ride."

"You look fit."

Mason looked very fit; he was solid and muscular, with no sign of superfluous fat. His white-yellow hair, lashes and almost invisible eyebrows, his bulldog face—blunt nose and square jaw, sanguine skin and wide mouth—certainly forbade handsomeness, but there was something about him. Life, zest, physical power and durability, easy good humour—these had captivated Florence Mason. They captivated her still. When Mason bent to kiss her lightly on the cheek, and Gamadge saw the look in her eyes, he knew that while her husband troubled to placate her she would never get rid of him. She might scold him, punish him, even hate him, but she would not do without him. Gamadge was sure that her rage at her own weakness was what made her implacable towards Bill and Sally Deedes. They, at least, should part! I could shake her, he thought, and listened to Mason.

"Now we'll get the mystery solved. Until a couple of days ago I didn't want you up here on the job, Gamadge—I'll be frank with you. I always think the less fuss made about these private rows the better. But I didn't like the tone of that last crack Florence found in her manuscript; the sooner we get rid of the joker now the better I'll be pleased."

Gamadge had relaxed into an easy posture, one hand in a trouser pocket and one shoulder drooping, which took an inch off his height; it permitted Mason to look down on him. "Can't promise results," he said. "The problem may be insoluble."

"Oh, don't give up before you start, old man! I'd hand you a tip to set you going, but Florence doesn't think much of it."

"I'll be glad of it, if you think it's worth something." Gamadge avoided Mrs. Mason's angry eye.

"Well, I'm a dumb sort of feller, only see what's in front of my nose; but it strikes me the joker is a neurotic. Not entirely responsible. Lots of young people are, and get over it. They write poison-pen letters, and a psychiatrist cures 'em."

"We've been over that, Tim," said Mrs. Mason coldly. "Mr. Gamadge doesn't think much of the idea, and he doesn't think much of Syl's, either—that I wrote the things in myself."

"You write 'em in? What nonsense. Just like Sylvanus,

though. He'd rather make Florence think she was going crazy, Gamadge, than have trouble in the home."

"And Henry says those things in my book are all quotations."

"Quotations?"

"Poe, and Christopher Marlowe, and I don't know who all."

Mason laughed heartily. "The spirits must have been taking a course in English Lit. We ought to tell Sally." He became grave, and added: "I hope to goodness you will clear the mess up, Gamadge; it's scaring fits out of my wife."

"Well, I've made a little progress; the spirits aren't responsible, and Mrs. Mason isn't responsible, and it wasn't a joke."

"Not a joke; you mean it was plain malice?"

"More than malice. I should say a flavour of madness."

"Oh, come now! If you're going to be an alarmist I won't go on thinking that you're a good doctor for my wife at all."

"At any rate, I prescribe company at night for her until she's less nervous."

Mason stood with his arms hanging at his sides, his brows knitted in what seemed perplexity. "You're not pretending she's in any danger, are you?"

"It's certainly dangerous to lose too much sleep. Of course she worries; so would you, so would I in her place."

"I wouldn't. I thought the best thing for Florrie's nerves would be to make light of the thing. I don't know why she didn't lock up her manuscript after that first happening."

"I'm rather glad that she didn't dam the flow," said Gamadge. "It might have burst forth in another place. Your wife oughtn't to be alone at night just now, Mason."

"Sally can come in. Unfortunately I'm no good as a cure for insomnia; I snore, I get up at seven, and I can't sleep a wink myself if my doors open."

"How about the faithful Louise?"

"Louise is as nervous as a witch herself. If Florence would

have the dogs—" he glanced down at the griffons. They sat side by side, looking from one speaker to the other as if interested in the conversation.

"And listen to them scratching at your door all night?" asked Mrs. Mason crossly. "No, thanks."

"Have Louise," said Gamadge.

Mason abandoned the subject without more words. He asked; "How are you going to start the investigation, Gamadge? Are you going to examine the old typewriter for fingerprints?"

"Fingerprints bore me. I'll begin by having a talk with you all after lunch—all but Florence; she's to absent herself from the conference, and I'll report to her afterwards. I might as well know at once where everybody is at night."

He went and opened the bedroom door. At the other end of the corridor a triple-arched window showed him the bare tops of beeches, a distant ridge of hemlock, a strip of pale, wintry sky. Towards the front of the house the main staircase faced him, rising to the upper floor, and on his immediate left a little passage ran, at right angles, to the back stairs. Four solid doors on the left, five on the right, and between them scenic wallpaper and oak panelling.

"I'm next to Florence, with a bath between," said Mason. "The next two doors on that side belong to cupboards, and then comes a guest room—yours, I believe—and then Syl's. There's a bath connecting them, too. Sally's across the hall, opposite Syl; her door is just beyond the stairs. She has her own bath, too."

"Not much like the old days," said Gamadge, "when we all had our highly decorated bowls and jugs."

"And splashers," laughed Mrs. Mason. "There are lots more bathrooms now. Next to Sally is the hall one, and then comes Susie Burt. She shares a bath with Evelyn Wing. Evelyn has the last room on this side, just beyond the back passage."

"Where is Mr. Percy?"

"Right above our heads," said Mason, with a look of hu-

morous resignation. "The large north-west room—with bath, of
course. He's well dug in."

"Now, Tim, you know I always love to have Glen here,"
protested Mrs. Mason, "and you know he'll soon be leaving for
his air-force training. He's just waiting for them to send for him."

"I hope they'll let me fly." said Mason. Florence's eyes suddenly filled with tears. Gamadge asked hastily: "What does Mr.
Percy do for a living, if he does anything?"

"Oh, he does," said Florence. "He's not at all well off, poor
boy. He writes, I think; doesn't he, Tim?"

"Advertising copy at present," replied Mason.

"Who else is upstairs?" asked Gamadge.

"There's the other little guest room—the south-west one,"
said Mrs. Mason, and all the servants' rooms, and a big bath.
Thomas used to be in the garage, you know, but now we've
moved him in here; he has the nicest little suite, with his own
bathroom."

"Eight bathrooms; that's something."

"Oh, we're very comfortable now at Underhill."

Physically, thought Gamadge. He said: "Well, see you at
lunch; I think," he added, pausing with his hand on the door-
knob, "that Syl was right; we may eliminate the servants from our
problem. Euclid would call them absurd."

He went into the hall. Mason closed the door after him, but
not in time to prevent the griffons from rushing out at his heels.
They turned down the back passage, made for the stairs, and
began to scramble up them, loudly barking. Gamadge saw that
their objective was a young or youngish woman who stood on the
top step of the dark and narrow flight.

His first impression—heightened by the fact that she
wore a thimble—was definite; that Florence had a visiting
seamstress in the house. But the calmness of the prolonged
look she gave him, the careless gesture with which, still meeting his gaze, she repressed the bounds of the griffons, and at

last something familiar in the shape of her round, bright eyes, made him readjust his ideas. She wore a grey cardigan sweater, a longish brown skirt, brown stockings, and black Oxford ties of unsportsmanlike cut; she was probably a native, but she was apparently a Hutter.

"Excuse me," said Gamadge. "Would you mind telling me who you are?"

"I'm Corinne Hutter."

"Stupid of me; I didn't know there were any Hutters except Florence and Syl."

"I'm their cousin. I'm the only other one there is."

Her voice had the regional twang, but it was not unpleasing. There was a note of dry humour in it, and as his eyes grew more accustomed to the dimness of the little hallway and stairs he saw that her smile was dry too. She had a high, domed forehead from which dark hair was drawn tightly back into a topknot; her nose was long, her skin colourless or sallow; she ought to have been plain, she was very nearly plain, but not quite. And she was not insignificant. Gamadge thought that with half a chance to develop it, she would have had a certain distinction that Florence and Sylvanus did not possess.

"Younger branch of the family?" he asked.

"Yes. My father was Joel Hutter."

"Florence didn't tell me you were staying in the house."

"They probably don't know I'm here to-day. I drive over sometimes to take a walk in the woods."

"Well! I've known the Hutters for twenty years, and I didn't know they had a cousin in these parts."

"There's nothing funny about that," said Miss Hutter, smiling her dry smile. "I live in Erasmus. I'm one of the librarians in the Erasmus library."

"Look here; my name's Gamadge, and I'm up here on some business for Florence Mason. I have to talk to everybody in the house. Shall I see you at lunch?"

"Oh, no. I never eat with the house-parties. I had my lunch before I came over."

"Can I talk to you now? This may be my only chance."

"Come on up."

Gamadge climbed the stairs and followed her into the little south-west corner room. He remembered it well as a cubbyhole into which last-minute guests had often been crammed; a neat little place, with muslin curtains at the windows—one of them now had a long rent in it, near the frill, and Miss Hutter's needle was sticking in it—and fumed-oak furniture. It was very much as it had been, even to the brass bed with its muslin valance and the blue rag carpet. A small table was laden with magazines, Miss Hutter's handbag, her driving gloves, and her knitted hat.

She sat down in a rocking-chair. Gamadge took a hard one in front of her, and so small was the floor space that their knees almost touched.

"You were going downstairs when I saw you," he said. "Had you an errand? I can wait while you do it."

"Just going down to find Louise and ask her for some finer thread," she told him. "It can wait." She took a small sewing kit from her pocket, unrolled it, and got out a spool of white cotton and a minute pair of scissors. While she removed the needle from the curtain and threaded it, Gamadge automatically produced his cigarette case.

"Have one?" he asked, offering it to her, opened.

"I don't smoke."

"Mind if I do?"

"Yes; but you can if you want to."

Gamadge, replacing the cigarette case in his pocket, remarked: "Incredible woman; if you were in my will I'd cut you out of it."

Miss Hutter looked up at him to ask coolly: "Who's been talking to you about wills?"

"Your cousin Florence has."

"You said you never heard of me."

"When you told me who you were I was immediately struck by the fact that you don't figure in her will."

"Or in Cousin Sylvanus's will, either." She calmly began to sew up the rent in the curtain.

"Some other financial arrangement?" asked Gamadge diffidently.

"I don't know why you're interested," said Miss Hutter, "but there isn't any other financial arrangement. My side of the family always got along without Uncle Nahum's money, and so do I."

"You still regard it as the late Nahum's money?"

"Yes, and so does everybody else. Cousin Florence and Cousin Syl just spend it."

Gamadge said, raising his eyebrows, "Your attitude is unusual—in these times."

"Our side of the family is kind of independent. I have enough money of my own to live on, and I have my salary."

"I feel it a privilege to know you, I really do."

Miss Hutter returned his amused look, and then said: "I was Cousin Florence's secretary and sort of housekeeper a good while ago—the first she had. Before she was married. It didn't work."

"Didn't it?" asked Gamadge gravely. "Too bad."

"We never had a fight. I like her, and I like Cousin Syl. I come here whenever I want to, and take walks and a nap. I guess the truth is Cousin Florence and I are too much alike. She wants her own way, and I don't like to be bossed. Besides, I wasn't the right person for the job. Cousin Florence needs somebody she can dress up, and show around, and play cards with."

"Like Miss Susie Burt?"

"Susie Burt isn't cut out for a secretary."

"Like Miss Evelyn Wing?"

"I guess Evelyn Wing is just about right for Cousin Florence."

Gamadge produced Chapter Nine from his pocket. He said: "You may be the disinterested observer I've been hoping for. When were you here last, Miss Hutter?"

"Two weeks ago to-morrow; that Sunday it cleared up after lunch. I wasn't coming, and then I did come. Had a nice walk."

"If you haven't been here since, you probably haven't heard about this tampering with Mrs. Mason's book."

"What book?"

"She's writing a novel."

For a moment Miss Hutter looked a trifle arch. Then she said: "I didn't know about it. How was it tampered with?"

"Somebody typed things into it at night, after Miss Wing finished work on it. Here you are; you'll find them for yourself. Begin at Page 83."

She fastened off her thread, stuck the needle into the curtain, and took the script from him. By the way she travelled through it, Gamadge saw that she needed no help in seizing the facts. At last she looked up at him. "It's the craziest thing I ever heard of. When did it start?"

"Middle of last week, ended on Wednesday night; because on Thursday Florence decided that she'd had enough, and yesterday she made Syl get hold of me."

"Are you a detective?" She looked at him with interest.

"No, just investigate things sometimes."

"I should think she *would* have had enough of it by the time she saw this last quotation."

"Thank Heaven somebody admits to knowing it is a quotation."

"Of course it's a quotation. They all are. Who says they aren't?"

"Not even Miss Wing seems to have said they were."

She frowned at him, and then at the script. "I don't know where they're from."

"But you immediately knew them for literature. Don't

you agree with me that any educated person ought to know that?"

Miss Hutter considered. Then she said, "Lots of people can't tell one kind of writing from another. This Demon thing—who wrote that?"

"Poe."

"I can't place that poetry, either."

"George Herbert—*A Paradox*."

"The others sound like old plays."

"Of course they do, and they are from old plays. Ford and Marlowe."

"I guess I'm like a lot of librarians they tell about—I know more names of books than what's in 'em."

"Can you suggest why any person should distress Florence by putting these things into her book?"

She ruminated, and at last inquired: "Who was here those nights?"

"Sylvanus, Mason, Mrs. Deedes, Miss Burt, Miss Wing, and Mr. Percy."

Again she pondered, turning the leaves of the script. "There's something about it," she said at last, "that looks worse than just spite work. But it might be spite work."

"You think so?"

"Well—if you've known Cousin Florence all that long time you know a good deal about her, don't you?" She looked up at him.

"A good deal."

"She likes all these people," (and Gamadge knew that Corinne Hutter would never come nearer than that to the word "love"), "likes some of them ever so much. But anybody that gets on her nerves, or makes her mad, or even if she's just feeling mad herself at something else—she'll take it out on them. She'll say something mean."

"How mean?"

"Pretty mean. She works herself up to thinking that they're

out for what they can get, and that they're making fun of her behind her back."

"Sylvanus isn't out for what he can get."

"No, and I guess she trusts him more than any of them. And
I don't think Glen Percy ever makes her mad, and she wouldn't
say anything mean to him if he did. She can't get many young
men to the house any more. Susie Burt doesn't go around with
young ones much, and Evelyn Wing doesn't seem to have any."

"But she takes it out of the others, does she?"

"Yes, and they don't go."

"Poor devils, they don't."

"They must feel pretty mean themselves, sometimes."

"Mean enough to do that?" Gamadge indicated Chapter
Nine.

"I wouldn't have said so." She added: "I've heard her say
things even to Cousin Sylvanus. When she didn't think he helped
enough with the expenses, and when he fights with Cousin Tim
Mason."

"Does she go for the paragon—Miss Wing?"

"I don't think she does much. I don't think Evelyn Wing
would stand it. But I did hear her say once that Evelyn Wing
needn't dress up for Cousin Tim Mason, because she wasn't his
type."

"Heavens!" Gamadge winced.

"I know it sounds pretty bad, but Evelyn Wing had sense;
she just lets things like that roll off her back."

"If I were Miss Wing, and Florence said a thing like that to
me, hanged if I wouldn't hit the ceiling. And if didn't hit the ceiling I might—" he put a forefinger on Chapter Nine, and looked
at Corinne Hutter inquiringly.

She thought it over. At last she said: "I don't think she's the
kind to do it; and even if she was, she'd do something else. This
typing, and these quotations and everything—they point to her.
She's too bright for that."

Gamadge said in an admiring tone: "You don't miss much. How about somebody wanting them to point to her?"

Corinne Hutter took this suggestion without surprise; but while she reflected on it she protruded her lower lip. She said at last: "I don't see much of them; just passing sometimes, and in Cousin Florence's room when I drop in to see her. I don't see them the way I used to when I was here all the time. Evelyn Wing wasn't here then. I don't know how they feel about her."

"They might be jealous, perhaps?"

"I don't know why they should. None of them can handle Cousin Florence, and they know it."

"Mason can't?"

"I hardly know him. I like him, though; he's always pleasant."

"This job—" Gamadge took back Chapter Nine, refolded it, and stowed it away again—"it's not a thing anybody could do—without help."

"Susie Burt couldn't."

"Could her friend Percy?"

"He reads a lot, anyway; he comes down to the library in Erasmus, and he sits with his feet up and reads for hours."

"What does he find to read there that he couldn't find in the excellent gentleman's library here at Underhill?"

"We have a fine library at Erasmus," said Miss Hutter, with some feeling. "It was a donation from some rich people that used to live there, and people give us their books. Somebody died in Bethea a few years ago and left us a thousand books, all old."

"What does Percy take out?"

"French poets and novelists, Old English poetry; dictionaries, and *The Anatomy of Melancholy*. He read that all one summer."

"Not for advertising copy, I am sure."

Miss Hutter gratified him by laughing.

"Sally Deedes couldn't do it alone," he went on, "but of

course Miss Wing's her cousin. And poor Bill Deedes could have helped her, but I don't see him at it."

"Besides, they're divorced now"

"So they are. Syl could do it, and Mason ought to be able to, unless he's forgotten that there's any printed matter outside of *Racing Form*. He went to a good school and university. And for all we know, somebody may have helped *him*."

She said, as he rose, "It's perfectly terrible to think of Cousin Tim Mason doing such a thing. It's perfectly terrible anyway. Mrs. Deedes never did it."

"Do you think she'd boggle at much, if she had an idea she'd be helping Bill?" He added, "Divorce or no divorce."

"I don t know why this should help Mr. Deedes. He's going to marry a rich widow."

"Well, we must confer about it again. You're invaluable to me, Miss Hutter."

"I have got to get back to Erasmus this afternoon."

"It's clouding over; don't miss your walk."

She cast a glance at an enormous and shining magazine that lay on top of the others. "I want to finish a story, first. We don't take many periodicals at the library."

As he reached the door the griffons came whiffing from under the bed. Gamadge, surprised at their emergence, remarked that they seemed to get around faster than the human eye could follow them.

"Just like lightning bugs," agreed Miss Hutter. "You never know where they're going to turn up." She admonished them: "Go down and get your lunch, now." They galloped past him to make for the front stairs; Gamadge went after them, and descended to the second floor.

CHAPTER FIVE

Planchette

SYLVANUS HUTTER'S LARGE CORNER ROOM communicated with one which had often been occupied by his young friends in times long past, and had been adapted to their muddy boots and casual ways. Now its serviceable drab-coloured curtains and rugs were replaced by fine chintz and broadloom, its Morris chairs and brass bedstead by rich old mahogany. Two charming oils of the Hudson River school graced the flowery walls, and yellow-glass ornaments, once relegated to the servants' quarters, had been recognized as period decoration and arranged respectfully on the mantelshelf.

Gamadge found that his things had been unpacked and put away. He washed up in the gleaming white bathroom, and then knocked at the communicating door. Receiving no answer, he went down to the library.

This was very much as it had always been; large and solemn, with tall and narrow windows framed in claret-coloured rep, a red Turkey carpet, and a huge black-marble mantelpiece. The old clock-and-vase set had gone from the mantel, however, and been replaced by an arrangement of Chinese bronzes; a slim lady twelve inches tall stood on her pedestal at either end of the shelf, swaying gently towards an antique bowl in the centre.

The clock had been moved to a console at the end of the room, between the windows. Gamadge was glad to see it there, and to hear, as he entered, its low, pleasant chime. But he was not sorry that the aquarium and the parrot cage had disappeared; Polly must at last have died, and the Hutters grown tired of reptiles in the home.

He wandered along the glass fronts of the bookcases, but found nothing that he sought until he reached a section to the right of an arched doorway that led into the den, now the office. He was taking books out of it when Sylvanus came in from the hall.

"What are you looking for?" Sylvanus approached, cigarette in hand.

"Edgar Allan Poe, George Herbert, John Ford, and Christopher Marlowe."

"Good gracious."

"I have Ford and Marlowe here."

"Poe's in this corner; Herbert? Herbert? Poet, is he?"

"Religious poet of the seventeenth century." Gamadge, turning the leaves of John Ford, did not look up at his host.

"Then he ought to be—yes, here he is. Here they both are. I have no wish," said Sylvanus quizzically, "to pry into the amusements of guests; but aren't you providing yourself with rather serious bedtime reading?"

"They provided the elegant extracts which were found in your Aunt Florence's novel. I wasn't sure of Ford, but here's one, and I'd swear that the other is in *The Broken Heart*."

Sylvanus turned from the corner bookcase, a red-brown volume in his hand. "They were quotations?"

"I should have thought the fact reasonably clear."

"Good gracious. To tell you the truth, Gamadge, I barely glanced at the things. I fought shy of them. I hoped everything would simmer down and come to nothing. Here's Herbert."

"Look up 'A Paradox,' and then Poe's 'Silence—A Fable.'"

They both turned pages. "Here we are," said Sylvanus at last. "'*Listen to me, said the Demon.*' Well, I'll be hanged."

"And here's the other Ford, in that piece whose title we have no concern with."

"No concern with it?"

"Oh, no; we never mention it. People can't make up their minds to produce it, because they can't imagine the title in front of a theatre in electric lights."

Sylvanus joined him, peered, laughed, and then grew grave. "I didn't even know we had a Ford. Good heavens— you think the party used our books!"

"What do you think?"

"Good heavens. Shall you examine them for fingerprints?"

"I wouldn't bother. Florence never wrote these quotations into her book, Syl; not even with the help of the spirits."

"I suppose not. Sally's been filling her up with a lot of mischievous nonsense, though, and I was afraid it had been too much for her nerves. I was afraid she might be splitting off a personality or something."

"Not Florence. Sally, perhaps, if she's the wreck you make out."

"She is. One doesn't like to scold her. One rather likes her to get what comfort she can."

"Where do they hold the séances?"

"In the office there."

"Does Miss Wing sit in on them?"

"Don't think so; she's a sensible girl, not like that at all."

"You really like her, don't you?"

"I do, very much," Sylvanus spoke sharply.

Gamadge piled the Poe and the Herbert on Ford and Marlowe. He said: "I had the pleasure of meeting your cousin Miss Hutter just now."

"Oh, is she here to-day?" Hutter laughed. "Quite a character, didn't you think?"

"Quite. She seems intelligent, too."

"Oh, very. We're quite fond of her, but you can't do much with—or for—that type. Just like her father. She loves to tell people that she won't be beholden to Florence and me."

"She told me so."

"Of course she did. Old Joel made her promise, or something. Of course Florence and I will eventually set up an annuity for her, whether she likes it or not. She can give it to the Erasmus library if she doesn't want it. But by that time she'll probably be delighted to have it; best room in the boarding-house, world cruises—if there are world cruises then. Her airs annoy Florence, but I think she really has a stiff kind of affection for us both."

"Let's have a look at the office." Gamadge picked up the books and followed Hutter into a narrow room with one window; it had a second door into the rear hall, and contained a large desk, a desk chair, filing cabinets, and a revolving bookcase. The space between the two doors was occupied by a bridge table and two small folding chairs; and on the bridge table stood a little heart-shaped object, mounted on two delicate wheels and an upright pencil.

"This place is smaller than it used to be," said Gamadge, looking around him.

"Oh, yes." Hutter raised the venetian blind as high as it would go, and pushed aside tan-coloured silk curtains. "We cut a chunk off the west side of it to make room for a new coat closet and downstairs dressing-room. We're very comfortable up here now. Game room in the basement; even Florence plays ping pong."

Gamadge laid the pile of books on the desk. He said: "Can we lock these up anywhere?"

"Why not with the rest of Florence's script?" Hutter pulled out a deep drawer. Gamadge deposited the books in it, locked it, and held out the key.

"Keep that. I only wish the script had been locked up every night, and then all this wouldn't have happened." Sylvanus uncovered a typewriter of somewhat ancient appearance. "We've been meaning to get a new machine for Underhill, and now, damn it, there are no more silents to be had."

Gamadge sat down at the typewriter, placed a fresh sheet of paper in it, and after a glance at Page 83 of Chapter Nine, wrote slowly with one finger:

SYLVANUS MASON FLORENCE SALLY BURT PERCY WING

"What's that for?" Sylvanus leaned over his shoulder.

"That's to show you that we shall never find out from this typewriter who wrote those quotations into Florence's book. They were typed slowly, with equal pressure, in caps."

"By Heaven, it was an ugly joke! Who did it, Gamadge? Who did it?"

"I don't know. I shall talk to the parties after lunch; but if you don't know, or can't guess, who did it, I doubt if I shall be able to."

"I'm absolutely in the dark!"

Gamadge looked up at him, smiled faintly, and slightly shook his head.

"No, but I am, Gamadge!"

"I believe you. Did you tell Florence that Miss Wing wasn't the guilty party?"

Sylvanus stepped back, flushing. "I—who said she was the guilty party? Ridiculous!"

"You see, you have no information for me, Sylvanus. I'm to go at it blind. Do you still hope that it will all blow over, and that after being scared off by me the guilty party will mend his or her ways for ever? And never be found out?"

Sylvanus hesitated, puckered up his mouth, and at last declared: "Yes! I do!" and stared defiantly at Gamadge.

"Although it was such an ugly joke?" He added, after a pause: "You're braver than I am, Syl; I confess I shouldn't want this joker in the house with me." Then, picking up another sheet of paper, he rose and went over to the bridge table. "So that's the oracle," he said, leaning forward to smile down at planchette.

"Beastly little thing." Sylvanus scowled at it.

"At least it can't use a typewriter."

"What a ghastly idea."

"I've never had a try at planchette. Have you?"

"I should hope not!"

"Sad to depart this life, Sylvanus, without knowing whether one's psychic or not."

"I bet I'm not."

"Let's try."

"I can't now; I must give Thomas the key to the wine cellar. I'll let you know when the cocktails are ready."

Sylvanus trotted into the hall. Gamadge closed the door after him, and the door to the library He then lowered the venetian blind, was not satisfied by the twilight he found himself in, and pulled the curtains together. He fastened them with a clip from the desk tray. Much better—the office was now in semi-darkness.

He returned to the bridge table, sat down with his back to the window, and placed his fingers on planchette.

A few minutes of waiting in dusk and silence made him reflect that ritual, properly conformed with, itself produces a sense of the reality supposed to exist behind the observance. He found himself definitely expecting some phenomenon not within the laws of nature; and when he began to be aware of a fullness in his fingers, and then a pressure against them, the material effort on him was that planchette had come to life. He knew that his arms were tired and that his fingers were weighing more heavily against the board, but, so far as his conscious perceptions were concerned, planchette was deliberately pushing at them.

And there was more to it than that. Without the slightest intention on his part, planchette was trembling, moving, sliding across the paper. Suddenly it shot off the paper entirely, and then shot back again. This process repeated itself several times, until at last Gamadge snapped on his lighter and investigated. He fully expected to see nothing but a scrawl, and that was what he did see; but a vicious-looking scrawl, which though it spelled no word seemed to mean something disagreeable, even dangerous.

He pushed planchette aside, turned the paper over, and got out a pencil. Then, placing his wrist lightly on the table, he closed his eyes; wondering if this game would be as unproductive of results as the other. It seemed totally unproductive of any result whatever. The table, it is true, pressed slyly and persistently against his hand, but nudged it in vain; for the hand apparently refused to take the hint and write anything.

Suddenly he became acutely uncomfortable in another way; something assailed his consciousness with a strong, definite warning, and he opened his eyes. He was looking with astonishment at a pale form, which seemed to float in a void. A face took shape, and dark caverns of eyes. He sat rigid for ten seconds, and then, relaxing, said cheerfully:

"Hello; that you, Sally?"

Mrs. Deedes came forward into the room. Her greying hair ceased to merge with the pallor of her face, and her face with her grey woollen dress. She said: "Dear Henry, how wonderful to see you again."

"These doors don't make a sound, do they?" He got up and went to the window. "Let me get a look at you, Sally."

"I'm not much to see, any more. Were you having a little séance all by yourself? How lovely."

"I'm no good at it." Having parted the curtains and raised the blind, he turned to survey her. He had once thought her beautiful, and her features were as fine, the poise of her head on its long neck was as graceful, as in the past. But the greying of her black hair aged her, and made her pale skin unearthly; it had the same tone as her antique pearl earrings and necklace, and the same purplish shadows.

The day was overcast. She stood in the pallid light, bending over the bridge table, a spectre of herself. But she spoke gaily:

"You say you're no good at it? Why, this is very nice, Henry. Did you do it with planchette?"

"Planchette? No, I didn't do anything with anything." He came to gaze with incredulity at a mincing line of words, run together without a break, which when separated formed the following mawkish invitation:

Goodwin come Goodwin come dance round the tree.

Gamadge, shocked, inquired: "Did I do that?"

"Of course you did. Was it automatic writing?"

"My hand never moved, and it's not my writing." Gamadge looked about him as if for the half-wit upon whom he might foist responsibility.

"It's never in one's own handwriting, and one's hand seldom seems to move. One doesn't do it one's *self*, Henry."

"I'm glad of that."

"Something takes hold."

"If a mosquito could write, that's the handwriting of a mosquito; but not even the spirit of a mosquito would bother to come back to earth and invite Goodwin to dance round a tree."

"It may not be a spirit, Henry. I'm not sure that the mischievous influence that has been troubling Underhill was ever on earth at all." She looked at him gravely.

"No elemental ever heard of Goodwin. Goodwin was a boy I used to know, and an earthy one. Goodwin belongs to my unconscious—I don't consciously think of him, I can tell you."

"The strangest things come through."

"You really think a malicious being of some sort wrote that fearsome stuff in Florence's novel?"

"Even the malicious ones can't hurt us."

"This one will probably end by hurting somebody severely in his or her finances. If I believed in them, Sally, I should hesitate to invite them into my life."

"But it's really rather gratifying; it shows that Florence is really in rapport."

"With the spirit world?"

"Of course."

Gamadge produced Chapter Nine. "Did you study these interpolations?"

"I saw each one once, after it came."

"Did they impress you at all? Did their rhythms fall upon your ear with any grandeur? Did they, in fact, damn it all, strike you as the sort of thing that could possibly originate with a being who would exhort Goodwin to dance round a tree?" Gamadge paused to draw breath.

"I don't know what you mean, Henry. That Demon one—"

"That Demon one is literary. Literary. Mine came from my kindergarten; Florence's were produced by four men of genius—Poe, George Herbert the seventeenth-century English religious poet, John Ford, and Christopher Marlowe—Elizabethan dramatists."

"You mean they are quotations?"

"They are."

"How very, very interesting."

"You think a spirit of any kind whatsoever would bother to

send somebody else's stuff through, via planchette or via that typewriter there?"

"Nobody knows what they'd do, Henry."

"You're just talking about spirits so that you won't have to think the thing out. I bet you have a notion who did it, which you won't admit even to yourself."

"I haven't any notion." She looked distressed.

"You've known all these people all these years."

"That's just it. None of them would play such a trick on Florence."

"Would they play such a trick on one another, though?"

"What?" she seemed dazed.

"I do wish you'd use your wits on it. They used to be good ones—must be good still, if you're able to run a dress shop and make it pay."

"It doesn't pay now, and I've changed since you knew me; I'm more than forty-five—I'm old and stupid. Did you hear that I've had to let Bill go?"

Gamadge had a sudden clear vision of Bill Deedes, his face calm and gay, vaulting over a tennis net. He said gently: "Yes. Too bad."

"I wish he had ever tried to get on with Florence. She's been awfully good to me, but she never cared much for Bill."

"People like Bill can't pretend, Sally."

"No."

Gamadge put Chapter Nine back into his pocket. "I'll have more to say after lunch. Do you suppose cocktails are ready? I could manage one, couldn't you?"

"I'm dying for one," said Mrs. Deedes.

CHAPTER SIX

Explosive

GAMADGE AND MRS. DEEDES LEFT the office by the door leading to the hall. Another door faced them, which belonged to a large cupboard under the stairs. This had always been crammed with hats, coats and overshoes, games and garden implements, skates, golf bags, archery bows and arrows, dog leashes and walking sticks; and it had smelled outrageously of rubber, leather, and lubricating oils.

Gamadge looked at it, and then looked over his shoulder at another door along the hall. "I suppose that's the new closet and dressing-room," he said.

"Yes, and it's such a comfort. It has racks for our coats, and there's even a little flower room and sink."

"This one must be quite cleared up."

Mrs. Deedes smiled. "It is. We can shut the griffons in here when they bark too much."

"They don't smother?"

"No, they like it."

"Like it?"

"They often rush in without being told to after they've been barking at plumbers."

"Really?" Gamadge stood looking down the hall, which ended in darkness and a swing door. A short passage corresponding to the one on the second floor led to the back stairs and the entrance to the cellar flight.

"Funnily arranged, Underhill," he remarked.

"Is it?"

"Don't you think so? It has only two entrances, front and back; and the back one is a continuation of this hall we're standing in. Or has it been changed?"

"No, it's just the same."

"With the kitchen on one side and the pantry on the other?"

"Yes. The dishes do have to be carried across the hall."

"And the only entrance to the dining-room is at the end of a transverse passage—with the servants' sitting-room opposite the kitchen at the other end?"

"Yes. What of it?"

"Poor Thomas."

Sylvanus Hutter appeared from around the front stairs. "There you are, you two," he said. "Cocktails."

Gamadge was delighted with the new drawing-room of Underhill; it had been formed from the old front and back parlours, and was now long and wide, with four windows to the north and two to the east. It was full of colour. Chinese flowers and birds were on the walls, on the soft-upholstered chairs and sofas, on the porcelains that contained dark red roses. "Nice, isn't it?" agreed Sylvanus.

"Lovely."

"Rather an improvement on the cabbage roses and the malachite. We've kept practically nothing but the mantelpiece."

They advanced on the group around that fine elevation of

white marble. Mrs. Mason sat in front of the fire in a bluish-purple costume, long and trailing; she had a cocktail glass in her hand, and beckoned to Gamadge with a festive sweep of it. The others looked at him.

"Come and meet people, Henry," she called. "But first get your drink, do."

Thomas and a large blonde maid supplied Gamadge with a cocktail and a canapé. He came forward, looking amiable.

"This is Susie Burt." A pretty girl with red hair, who stood behind the sofa talking to Mason, nodded. "You knew her mother," continued Mrs. Mason. "Susie, Mr. Gamadge knew your mother."

"And father," said Gamadge.

Miss Burt, who did not reach to Mason's shoulder, turned large blue eyes on him. They had a fine, bold gaze, more mature than one would have expected at first sight of her round face, with its delightful nose that turned up and its childlike mouth that turned down. But a second glance told Gamadge that she was in her late twenties. Wish I could have seen her ten years ago, he thought, returning the blue stare with one of benevolence.

"How do you do?" said Miss Burt. She did not look as though she cared to be cherished on account of her parents.

"Miss Wing," said Mrs. Mason, "Mr. Gamadge."

A dark girl with a pale face bowed to him. A thin face it was, with delicate features; and her eyes, after all, were not dark but grey-blue. Her thick, fine hair was cut short, and made a long neck seem longer. She wore tweeds and a yellow-silk shirt.

Good at sports, thought Gamadge, noting the long, well-muscled figure and the easy pose of it. Or was, he added, until she got ill and then had to work for a living indoors. Seen trouble.

"How do you do?" said Miss Wing, and turned her eyes away.

"And Glen Percy," said Mrs. Mason, with a smile for the

dark young man who stood with his elbow on the mantelshelf. "He's a perfect darling when he's behaving himself, and you'll simply love him."

"What I say is," said the young man in a tone of deprecation, "let's keep our heads, even if we are tight."

"You horrid child, I am not tight!"

Gamadge was not quite sure of it; Mrs. Mason was undoubtedly bolstering up her courage with the aid of excellent Martinis. She took another from the tray, as Gamadge shook hands with Mr. Percy and looked at him with some interest.

Percy's voice had proclaimed him a Southerner, and something—some elegance, some native languor that was probably by no means a languor of the spirit—belonged to the Southern legend. But he had an ironic humour; it showed in the tone of his drawl, the droop of his eyelids and his mouth. He was one of the handsomest young men Gamadge had ever seen. His face and his long hands were slightly tanned, his tweeds and shoes of English cut and by no means new.

He had been talking, or trying to talk, to Miss Wing; but the secretary seemed to wish to ignore him; he was forced to address the back of her head.

"…allergic to it," he went on, as Gamadge turned away. "Completely allergic to it. So at the dance I said: 'My dear girl, you'll have to take it off.' She took it off, and caught the most fearful cold, and was in bed for a week. I warned her—I can't be within a mile of Angora, but she would wear the thing. I don't mind other furs so much, but I always feel the effects of a long session with disguised rabbit."

Gamadge glanced at Miss Wing; she was still oblivious of Percy, or seemed to be, and he addressed his further remarks to Mrs. Mason: "I wish you'd call these creatures off, I really do. Somebody's been giving them bacon, and they're getting it on my shoes." He looked down at the griffons, which were pawing him.

"Now, Glen, they're so devoted to you!"

"And I'm devoted to them, when they don't dribble. They remind me of a monkey I once had; Susie, do you remember Tinkabella?"

Miss Burt also seemed to be annoyed with Mr. Percy. She glanced away from Mason long enough to say: "No, I certainly do not," and then looked back at Mason again.

Gamadge met the dark, glinting eyes. "You are fond of Barrie?" he inquired with gentle interest.

"Barrie?"

"Your pet's name is somewhat reminiscent..."

Percy, with a stricken look, warded off the suggestion with a long, bronzed hand. "Please," he begged. "Don't misjudge me like that. I never dreamed of such a—I am completely allergic to *Peter Pan*."

Luncheon was announced. Gamadge, finding himself at the end of the procession with this young man who wished to be thought a silly ass, wasted no time.

"You perhaps know that I'm here on business, Mr. Percy," he said.

"Glad you are here," said Percy civilly, "no matter why. I did understand that you were to be consulted about the poltergeist."

"I'm trying to get you people sorted out."

"Morally or intellectually?" Percy smiled at Gamadge.

"Just your relationships at first. Do I gather that you are here as a friend of Miss Burt's?"

"Susie and I are old friends, sure enough; but it would be more accurate to say that I'm here because her parents and my parents were great friends. When I was left alone in the world Mrs. Burt used to look more or less after me; not financially, of course—we all had money then. Excuse my mentioning the word; I'm completely allergic—" he stopped, and added as they went into the glittering, mirrored dining-room: "I don't know why I keep on using that repulsive phrase. I've been saying nothing else all day."

"Perhaps you're like me," said Gamadge. "I always become inane when I have something on my mind."

The black eyes swivelled towards him. "Whatever else you do to us," he implored, "don't psychoanalyse us. I'm com—I mean it's a game I have no confidence in."

"I have no qualifications for playing it," said Gamadge.

As he stood waiting to take his place between Miss Burt and Evelyn Wing he caught a glimpse of Corinne Hutter starting out on her walk. She came around the back of the house and passed the west and then the north windows; doubtless on her way to the old trail, up the hill that sheltered the Hutter place and gave it its present name. She plodded stoutly forward, a self-contained small figure in a cheap plaid coat.

"She'll get rained on, I'm afraid," said Gamadge. Miss Burt, following his glance, remarked that that hat could stand it, and then sat down and began to talk to Sylvanus Hutter; who, rather to Gamadge's surprise, was at the end of the table opposite Florence Mason. Mason sat at her left hand.

Miss Wing proved a pleasant, if reserved, table companion. She talked readily about books and plays, but seemed to have missed seeing *Julius Caesar* in modern dress, the more recent *Hamlet*s, and a memorable performance of *Doctor Faustus*.

When at last Miss Burt turned to him, she responded to his conversational efforts without animation. She had put Gamadge down as merely benevolent, and therefore a weariness and a waste of time.

"Mrs. Mason says you used to be her secretary, Miss Burt," said Gamadge at last.

"I was no good at it. I never could type properly, and I never was any good at arithmetic."

"I'd forgotten the typing. I can't type properly myself, never shall."

"Neither shall I."

"Do you use one finger, as I do?"

"Yes, and I break my nails."

The nails in question were lacquered cunningly to match her hair; Gamadge, looking at them with awe, asked: "What do you like to do?"

"I like to play bridge. Now that you're here I hope we can get up two tables. It's so awful cutting in."

"I can only stay until to-morrow."

"To-morrow!" She looked surprised and pleased.

"Yes. Pretty hopeless, solving this problem of the typescript in that length of time?"

"It was just a joke; nobody will ever find out who did it."

"You don't know me. What are you doing now, Miss Burt? When you're in town, I mean."

"Nothing. There aren't any jobs. Mrs. Mason wanted Mrs. Deedes to give me one in her shop, but there's no room. I wanted to try for the movies long ago, but Mother wouldn't let me, and now I'm too old."

"Mr. Percy ought to be in the movies."

She cast a black look across the table at Percy, and said: "*He* couldn't act."

"Not even in private?"

"In private he could—with girls. You know how Southern men are."

"No; how are they?"

"I mean with girls. They always behave as if they were in love with them all."

"Rather charming."

"I think it's horrid."

"I mean, if the girl isn't taken in. I thought Southern men were still rather punctilious about taking people in."

"They're worse than anybody."

Luncheon had come to an end. Florence rose, everybody rose; but she did not lead the way out of the dining-room; instead, she looked truculently at her guests, and made a short and shocking speech—the thought hers, but the words dictated by her three cocktails:

"I'm going to have my coffee upstairs, and you're to have yours in the big room. Mr. Gamadge is going to ask you questions; he's going to find out who put those things into my novel. He knows I didn't, and he knows the spirits didn't; that's nonsense. He thinks it was a horrible thing to do, and if anybody doesn't wish to answer his questions and help him find out who did it, that person can stay out of the room; but that person needn't stay in the house."

Blank faces confronted her; but Sylvanus, greatly embarrassed, was the only one of the party who spoke:

"Florence. Please."

"I'm not going to be polite about it. I mean everybody."

Mason looked aghast. He stood gripping the back of his chair, his eyes fixed on his wife.

"I'm serious about this," said Florence, "and it's time you all were, too. For your own sakes, you'd better do what you can to help him get to the bottom of it."

She walked around the table, and out of the room by the side door. The two griffons, gambolling after her, tumbled on and off her train. She paid no attention to them, and sent no backward glance to her stupefied family and guests.

When the door had closed—pretty sharply—behind her, Sylvanus muttered: "She's all upset," and led the way into the drawing-room. The others trooped silently in his wake, and Thomas, with the coffee tray, got them over the first moments of shock. There seemed at first to be some question whether or not Mason would plunge out of the room after his wife; he stood irresolute, looking out into the hall, until Thomas approached him. Then, however, he seized a cup from the tray and gulped hot coffee down. But he remained standing beside the doorway.

Miss Burt, after a long look in his direction, went and sat at the end of the sofa not occupied by Mrs. Deedes. Miss Wing took a low chair at some distance from that lady, and Percy resumed his earlier position at one end of the hearth; he placed his cup on the ledge of the mantel. Sylvanus wandered up and down, muttering.

"Had no idea she felt so strongly," he said; and then, confronting Gamadge, "You must have worked her up."

"I hope so; I meant to." Gamadge walked to the other end of the hearth, got out Chapter Nine, and faced the room.

"Mrs. Mason's speech," he began, "seems to me to need no apology. A wretched trick has been played on her, a trick which appals me far more than it appals her. It demands the most serious consideration. It wasn't a joke, you know, although the perpetrator certainly wished to amuse him- or herself as well as to frighten the victim."

Percy took a sip of coffee, and got out a cigarette. "Are you sure, Mr. Gamadge," he asked with detachment, "if you know how insensitive the practical joker can be?"

"The effect is brutal," said Gamadge, looking at him, "but it is not humorous. Please note that the additions to the text are not parodies, they are not even comments on it; they are merely echoes. The first and last don't do more than achieve a certain verbal continuity; they don't fit into the sense of the text at all."

"To have fitted them into the sense of the text," said Percy; "would have taken some doing."

"You put your finger on an important point." Gamadge continued to look at the young man. "A most important point. What *was* done took some doing; for our friend had to do it all— choose the quotations, you know, before writing them in—after Miss Wing herself had finished work for the evening; for who, except Miss Wing herself, could have known where she would leave off?"

Sylvanus came up to the back of the sofa and gripped it with both hands. He gazed fixedly at Gamadge, his eyebrows drawn together in a frown.

"Opportunity," Gamadge went on, "was therefore not so free as it seems. None of the work could be prepared in advance. Our friend had to wait until everybody was upstairs and presumably asleep; too well settled, in fact, to wander forth again and be surprised at the activities of a midnight reader—no typing would I think be heard through those doors. Our friend had first to consult the typescript, and then go into the library and hunt up a quotation that could be used first with arresting, then with terrifying effect; for each is more threatening than the last.

"So much for the literary part of the job. But what about the technical part? Don't underrate the skill that went into this piece of work—these five pieces of work. The page was replaced in the typewriter, and the quotation inserted; with no erasures, with no faults, and with professional spacing and alignment; each interpolation is put in exactly as the others are. I'm a mere amateur at the typewriter, much as I've used it; and I couldn't possibly have done this job."

Mason spoke suddenly from the other side of the room: "Of course whoever did it knew how to type and knew about books."

"There," said Gamadge, "I think you're wrong. This person need not have known much about books; the literary end of the job required no more than patience, and the bare knowledge that pertinent material could be found in Poe, in the cryptic poems of the seventeenth or any other century—for poetry is a mine of the cryptic—and in the Elizabethan drama. A semi-literate person, I grant you, would have been more likely to resort to the Bible and Shakespeare; unless, of course, the attention of such a person had been called to these authors in some special way."

He ended with a rising inflection; then, after a pause, he went on:

"But I confess that I should have expected you all to know that the quotations were quotations. Miss Burt has forgotten how to use a typewriter, Miss Wing is not well acquainted with

Marlowe's *Faustus*, Mrs. Deedes thinks that the whole thing was the work of spirits, and so on; but I really should have thought that all of you—not to mention a literary man like Sylvanus, or an inveterate reader like Mr. Percy—"

Sylvanus interrupted, flushing deeply: "I explained. One becomes an ostrich. One refuses to admit *anything*."

"Why?" asked Gamadge.

Evelyn Wing, her eyes on the fire, her elbows on her knees, spoke drily: "It was silly of me not to say they were quotations. I knew they must be, of course. But I knew they all thought I had typed them in myself, and when you're in a jam you do silly things; at least I did."

Gamadge turned his eyes on Percy, who said, waving his cigarette in a gesture of negation, "Absolutely none of it was any of my business. I kept quietly out of it."

Miss Burt laughed—shrilly. Gamadge, his eyes once more on Page 83 of Chapter Nine, went on without emphasis:

"Miss Wing is of course the logical suspect, if one can imagine a motive for her. She is highly educated, she must know the books in this library pretty well—and I may say now that all our four authors are to be found in it—she is familiar with the typewriter's art, and—as I intimated before—she had the supreme advantage of knowing where she was going to stop; or, perhaps I should say, of stopping where Mrs. Mason's line would fit a line already chosen from the classics. Miss Wing, and Miss Wing alone, could adapt the text to the quotations instead of laboriously adapting the quotations to the text."

Percy, his cigarette in mid-air, said almost gaily: "Such an intelligent man! Is he going to disappoint me, or is he going to demolish this airy structure in the logical way?"

"It has been demolished," said Gamadge. "Mrs. Mason was at first inclined—for her own reasons, no doubt—to imagine that her secretary had made a mockery of their work together. But before I pointed out the obvious to her she had had it pointed out by someone else: Miss Wing herself would not have played a trick that she might readily be suspected of playing."

"Mrs. Mason ought to have seen something more obvious than that," said Percy, with a smile, "and seen it for herself. Miss Wing would never play such a trick at all."

"In fact," asked Gamadge, "you agree with me that the trick may possibly have been played by someone less highly qualified to play it than Miss Wing, but endowed with natural cunning, and perhaps assisted by an intelligent friend?"

"I agree with you," said Percy, looking amused.

Susie Burt sprang to her feet. "Well, I don't!" she exclaimed. "I don't agree with anything you've been saying. You think Evelyn Wing wouldn't do such a thing, Glen Percy? You think she's above it? She's done plenty of other mean things, I can tell you! She spies on us all. She told Mrs. Mason that Mr. Hutter drinks, and that Mr. Mason took me to a night club, and that you tried to make love to her!"

"That I tried to make love to Mrs. Mason?" Percy's expression was one of extreme horror.

"To Evelyn Wing," shouted Miss Burt. "And if I wanted to be so mean I could tell Mrs. Mason worse things than that!"

CHAPTER SEVEN

Lull in the Storm

MRS. DEEDES WINCED; SHE COWERED back against the sofa cushions, and put her hands over her ears. Mason strode across the room as if he were in his wife's novel, and roared: "Susie, will you be quiet?"

Susie Burt sank down; Percy wagged his head at her. "Who told you Miss Wing told Mrs. Mason all that?" he asked.

"Never you mind."

"I do mind. I deduce our dear faithful old Louise Baugnon, who is so fond of us all. Fond of us all," he repeated, smiling, "but with no respect for white-collar jobs."

Mrs. Deedes rose. "If you don't mind, Henry," she said in a feeble voice, "I shall go upstairs and lie down. I don't believe Florence meant us to listen to this kind of thing."

"No, no, Sally; wait a minute." Sylvanus gently urged her back upon the couch, and then turned to Miss Burt. "You ought to be made to apologize, Susie. What's the matter with you?"

"I won't apologize." Her voice trembled. "Glen Percy is putting it on me!"

Percy, with his eyes fixed on the top of Miss Wing's smooth head, remarked that all the theories originated with Mr. Gamadge.

Miss Wing had not moved. She sat looking at the fire, her hands clasped on her lap. Mason, with a glance at her, snarled: "You needn't come out with a lot of stuff about the rest of us, just to get even with Percy."

"I haven't come out with half I know!" Susie began to cry, a blue linen handkerchief pressed to her face. Percy addressed Gamadge mildly:

"May I remove this emotional wretch from the Presence, or is the conference still on?"

"It's off."

"Then I'll take her for a walk. I'm going out myself; I feel the need of a change of air."

Susie Burt started up, said in a choking voice that she never wished to speak to Percy again, and rushed out of the room. Mrs. Deedes rose, watched her go, and then slowly followed; her face expressed fastidious dislike.

Mason said hoarsely: "I never heard anything like it. Florence encourages a lot of half-bred youngsters to hang around looking for treats and *pourboires*, and this is the result—a bear garden."

"You're as bad as any of them!" Sylvanus turned upon him with spirit. "Why don't you set an example? And if you mean to include Percy and Miss Wing, you'd better apologize! If you don't, Florence shall hear of it—she'll be very angry."

"I bet she'll hear of it anyway," replied Mason. "As for that old witch of a Louise, I'll get rid of her; she's always running to Florence with backstairs gossip."

Sylvanus looked at him squarely: "There's been enough of trying to get rid of people, Mason."

"What do you mean by that?" Mason swung to confront him.

"I mean that Florence isn't to be further upset. As for carrying tales, so far as I know everybody in the house does it except myself and Miss Wing."

"Thanks," said Percy, and the word had a clear, warning note like the sound of a bell.

"I don't mean you; you're out of it," said Sylvanus, irritably.

"You mean I have nothing to gain from Mrs. Mason? Well," said Percy, with a smile, "there are treats, even if there are no *pourboires*."

"Mason shall apologize."

"I'm not taking orders from you, Hutter." Mason clenched and unclenched his fists. "You're not the master of this house."

"Perhaps not; but while I live in it there'll be decent behaviour in it." Sylvanus was magnificent. "If Florence wishes me to go elsewhere, she has only to say so."

"If this kind of thing goes on I'll leave myself. The place has struck me as being overcrowded for some time." Mason plunged from the room, and, apparently, straight from the house; the front door was immediately heard to slam with a noise like thunder.

After a dead silence lasting for thirty seconds at least, Gamadge asked faintly: "Won't he catch his death of cold with no hat or coat?"

"He never catches cold." Sylvanus fanned himself with his handkerchief. "He's proud of it. Miss Wing, let me thank you for your forbearance; nobody places reliance on the wild statements of our absurd Susie."

Evelyn Wing answered without turning her head: "She was just hitting out because she thought her friends were letting her down. I can hardly blame her."

"Don't be too good to be true," Percy begged her. "Mr. Gamadge looks to me like a man who would view too much altruism with suspicion."

"He doesn't look cynical enough," replied Miss Wing, "to think everybody is always playing a part."

"The allusion is to me," said Percy raising an eyebrow at Gamadge. "I'm the kind of fellow they wrote maxims about. 'There is something not entirely displeasing to us in the headaches of our patrons.' You know the kind of thing."

"That's a new one," said Gamadge, with a smile.

"A variation merely. Well, I'll have my stroll—unless it begins to rain; Mrs. Mason and I are developing ideas about the spring plantings in the walled garden."

He sauntered from the room. Miss Wing continued to look at the fire; Sylvanus interrupted his uneasy patterings up and down, to and fro, and stopped beside her. "Is Louise responsible for that stuff Susie gave us?" he asked.

"I don't know. Even if she were," said Evelyn Wing, "I shouldn't be inclined to judge her severely. It's easy to call people gossips and mischief-makers, but when they're in a dependent position what are they to do if they're questioned? Refuse to answer? Would that improve matters?"

Gamadge studied what he could see of her profile. A face difficult to read; was it an honest one? She had withheld knowledge, she had tried to mislead him at lunch-time; she had had years of diplomatic training in the service of Florence Mason. And she had kept the job—a job that Corinne Hutter had resigned or been dismissed from, a job that Susie Burt hadn't cared to work at. Evelyn Wing had been a success at it; did she know how great a success?

Sylvanus resumed his pacing of the room. "Hang it all," he protested, "I have my highball every night when I go to bed; and because Grandfather Hutter ended by getting too fond of his toddy, Florence will have it that I'm a secret tippler."

"I didn't tell Mrs. Mason that," said Evelyn Wing, her lips curving a little.

"Or any of the other things; of course you didn't." Sylvanus, again coming to a standstill, asked with a sidelong glance at her: "Is the Burt-Percy engagement broken again?"

"I don't know."

"Looks that way. They exchanged vows at the age of eight or thereabouts, Gamadge, and since then nobody ever knows whether the affair is on or off. I suppose Percy isn't such a fool as to have made a row about—er—Mason and the night club?"

"I don't know," said Miss Wing.

Gamadge remarked that he ought now to report to Florence.

"Just come and have a word with me first." Sylvanus grasped his elbow. "No, Miss Wing, don't move; we'll go into your office."

When they had reached that sanctuary Sylvanus closed both its doors and faced Gamadge peevishly. "Hanged if I don't think that whole shindy was your fault," he said.

"Of course it was. I had to stir them up; you wouldn't give me information, so I jounced it out of *them*." He added: "I suppose Mason is having some kind of affair with little Burt?"

"Utter nonsense! He goes to town oftener than Florence does, and she gets touchy and suspicious here with not enough to do, and so he keeps things from her; the most innocent things. Of course they ought to have told Florence they'd been out."

"I suppose if he didn't tell, Miss Burt couldn't."

"As for Percy, he may have tried to flirt with Miss Wing in order to get even with Susie for the Mason outing. Idiots."

Gamadge said: "To me the situation doesn't seem to be on that plane at all."

"Don't start exaggerating things."

"Miss Wing doesn't look like a girl one tries to flirt with un-invited."

"Nonsense. She's a bit grim just now; all this bother. And she means to keep this job—I told you she's had a taste of poverty. But she had plenty of social experience before her people died, they were rolling at one time—had a big place outside of Philadelphia. I hope she cuts a bit loose on vacations; not that she gets too many of those—when the time comes Florence always needs her for something or other, and gives her a watch or a fur coat instead. I sometimes think the girl's worked half to death."

Gamadge, who stood looking down at the typewriter, said: "I wonder if you noticed something; nobody seems to have carried tales to Florence about Sally Deedes or Evelyn Wing."

"Evelyn Wing?"

"The accusation about the script of the novel wasn't talebearing."

"Probably nothing to tell. Or Susie may be keeping some more scandal up her sleeve; she said she wasn't showing us the whole bag—little wretch!"

He stopped beside the bridge table and looked down at planchette; then, with a half-smile, he laid the fingers of one hand on it.

"Going to have your sitting now?" asked Gamadge.

"Uncanny little thing, isn't it? How do you work it? What do you do?"

"Just put all your fingers on it and wait."

"How long?"

"Till it writes, or you get sick of it."

Sylvanus, with a satirical grimace at his own expense, sat in the chair Gamadge had occupied, and followed the latter's directions.

"You ought to be in the dark," said Gamadge. "The spirits prefer it." He let the venetian blind down, and grey twilight enveloped the plump face and figure of Sylvanus. He drew the curtains.

"Come back after you've seen Florence," Sylvanus murmured. "I'll have a message for you. Solve the case."

"I'm going to give her some advice, and you must help me make her carry it out. See you later." Gamadge went into the hall, closing the office door behind him. He walked down to the swing door, and pushed a bell set into the wall beside it. Thomas looked out.

"Sorry to bother you, Thomas," said Gamadge. "Is Louise in there?"

"Yes, sir. She's in our sitting-room."

Gamadge looked at his watch. "It's ten minutes to three. Mrs. Mason wanted to see me, but doesn't she rest at this time in the afternoon?"

"Yes, sir, she does. But if she expects you—"

"I thought Louise might find out whether I'm to go now or wait."

Thomas withdrew, and Louise quickly arrived through the swing door. She was a French Swiss, who had taken care of Florence Mason for forty years. Wrinkled and yellow, in a neat black dress and without cap or apron, she looked what she was— an old-fashioned, obstinate, faithful, not very good-tempered lady's maid. She had no prejudice against the male sex, and greeted this member of it with a smile.

"Meester Gamadge! It is like old times!"

"Splendid to see you again, Louise." Gamadge put a hand under her arm and propelled her down the side passage. "Remember how you used to give us the dickens for tracking snow up these back stairs?"

"You were always a good nice boy."

"I still am. I want a word with you. I'm anxious about Mrs. Mason; she sent for me, you know."

"Zose *zings* in her book!" Louise allowed him to assist her up the steep flight.

"Yes. Come on down to my room and let's talk it over." As they entered, the griffons tumbled through the bathroom, yapping loudly, and made for the door. Gamadge, before closing it, gazed after them. "Going down the way we came up," he said. "They act as if they had an appointment."

"Sweet little zings. Always together," said Louise fondly. "Zey cannot find Mr. Hutter in his room, so zey look for him somewhere else."

Gamadge established her in an armchair, sat opposite her, and got out a cigarette. She smilingly watched him light it.

"Now," he said, "do for pity's sake help me. Who in the world could have put the things in Mrs. Mason's book? Who would?"

Louise's gnarled face became enigmatic. She said: "Some people would like to frighten a lady like mine. Zey are jealous, zey don't like to work for zeir living, zey would be ladies zemselves."

"Do it just for spite, would they?"

"And to make Madame turn everybody else away."

"Except you."

"Zey would turn me away if zey could."

"And you think some woman must have done it, do you?"

"No man would do such a zing!"

"Think not?" Gamadge, smoking, looked at her. Then he said: "You sound as if you know who the viper is. Have you warned Mrs. Mason?"

"She laughs at me, then she is angry. She tells me I cannot prove it, I will get into trouble."

"Not with me, you won't. Who is it?"

Louise shook her head. "I promised Madame I would never say what I think." She added: "Poor Mr. Mason."

"Poor Mr. Mason?"

Louise's nose twitched.

"Is he poor because he's taken in by this woman," asked Gamadge, "or because he is in danger from her, or because he can't get Mrs. Mason to listen to him, either—when he tries to warn her?"

Louise said: "Madame is not fair to Mr. Mason. He amuses himself, he is not old. Why should he not be happy?"

"Very odd how these stories get about to his wife."

"No, it is not odd," declared Louise, again looking enigmatic. "I know how zey get about, but Madame will not permit me to tell."

"Naturally they don't get about through you."

Louise was offended. "Me! I never carry tales to Madame."

"Not even to protect her against schemers?"

"No, never."

Gamadge, contemplating her with benign scepticism, asked: "Does Mr. Percy need protection too?"

"Meester Percy?"

"From the mysterious menace who has cast her spells on Mason?"

Louise was entertained by the notion. "He can take care of himself, zat one!"

"You sound as if you liked him."

"I love to have him come here. He is so funny, and he is such a gentleman. His clothes, zey fall apart, zey are so old, but he tips us all as if he were millionaire." She added: "And *beau comme le jour.*"

"Beautiful as the day; this day, perhaps—dark, you know."

Louise did not follow this, and Gamadge, certain that he would get no definite information from her except as to her predilection for the males in the house, rose from his chair.

"See if Mrs. Mason is ready for me, will you?" he asked. "I'm to report to her on all these people."

Louise got up too, looking defiant. "You may tell her what I say!"

"Don't think I shall even mention your name."

He followed her to Mrs. Mason's door, and waited while she knocked gently and went in. When she came out she was smiling. "Madame says what has become of you, she is tired of waiting!"

"She doesn't want to see me any worse than I want to see her."

A bright fire cast orange lights on the white woodwork of the fireplace; Florence, again on her chaise-longue, had a large illustrated book of gardens across her knees. It slid away as she half turned to address him eagerly:

"How did it go? How did it go?"

"I put them all in a temper."

CHAPTER EIGHT

Elemental

MRS. MASON SEEMED PLEASED at this news. She slightly tossed her head, and remarked that she wished she had been there.

"Now I'm going to make you lose *your* temper," said Gamadge.

"Mine?"

"I'm going to scold you, warn you, and give you some advice."

Mrs. Mason looked affronted, then alarmed. She said: "Why, Henry, what have I done?"

"I don't entirely know." He glanced about the room; seldom had he seen a more delightful one, with its long azure draperies, its pale-gold sheen of satinwood, its silvery walls. The twin beds, luxuriously appointed and supplied each with its blue-and-rose eiderdown, had a pair of night tables between them, with tambour-fronted drawers, silver reading lights and crystal ash trays.

In the north-west corner of the room stood a desk, its shallow pigeon-holes bulging with bills and letters.

Gamadge sat down beside Mrs. Mason, and looked at the desk, which was almost directly behind her.

"You always make a rough draft of a will, I suppose," he said.

"Oh, yes; several. Why?"

"Where do you keep the drafts until you're ready to draw up the will?"

"I don't know. In my desk, I suppose; my desk in New York, or this."

"This last will, the one Macloud wouldn't draw up for you—where did you put the draft of it, and where's the will?"

"There in the desk behind you."

"Macloud has the earlier one?"

"Yes. He always told me I mustn't put a will in a safe deposit box, because the tax men—"

"I know. Where did you keep the copies of the earlier wills you made—since your marriage?"

"In my desk in New York, Henry." Mrs. Mason was irritated.

"Do you keep that desk locked, and do you keep this one locked when you're out of the room?"

"No, because somebody always is in my room; I am, or Louise is."

"I suppose you don't relieve each other like sentries?"

"No, but people don't come in and hunt through my papers. They wouldn't dare. I wish you wouldn't look at me like that."

"How can I look at you?"

"Bob always told me the copy must be accessible."

Gamadge lighted a cigarette. "What it comes to," he said, "is this: any of your circle may have read the draft or the copy of any of your wills, and may have read this newest will itself."

"They wouldn't even know where to look!"

"Give me one minute at it—that's all." He smoked for a time in silence. Then he said: "I'm amazed that it hasn't occurred to you: somebody may have seen that twenty-five thousand dollar legacy to Miss Wing in the will you made three years ago, and seen that she wasn't exactly losing favour with you, and decided to get rid of her before you drafted another will, leaving her more."

"I tell you that until this happened about my book, I never dreamed people would go snooping around!"

"But Miss Wing's enemy proved to be her best friend; 'a paradox,'" said Gamadge, smiling. "Instead of being ruined with you, she is your residuary legatee. What if somebody has discovered that?"

"Henry, you frighten me; you really do!"

"Didn't Bob Macloud explain to you what would happen if you and Sylvanus should be killed in the same automobile accident, or bombed by the same Jap?"

Mrs. Mason shrank back among her cushions.

"Didn't he remind you," asked Gamadge, "that if Sylvanus predeceased you by only half a minute, and could be proved to have done so, your residuary legatee would inherit not a mere hundred thousand dollars odd and Underhill, but your father's millions?"

"Yes, but it's so unlikely, and this will is only provisional. I told him so!"

"Provisional—until you're sure Mason didn't write those extracts into your book. If he did, you'll show him this will and have your revenge?"

"How else could I make him realize what he'd done?"

"Poetic justice; it must be a lovely thing to play with. Mason may have seen these wills, Florence, or copies of them, or drafts of them; Miss Wing may have seen them."

"I tell you—"

"This tampering with your book seems to me a symptom,

rather than a fact to be taken by itself. The symptom of a rising crisis. You tell me people won't do this or that; I tell you that you don't know how people will react to stimuli such as you have provided them with by making those wills. I want you to make another one, Florence."

"Another? When?"

"To-day. I want you to make it, keeping in mind the fact that your residuary legatee may inherit the Hutter fortune; and the fact—you can face it, you know—that we're all mortal; that life is uncertain; that you might very well die without opportunity to change a will, or even express a wish in connection with it."

Mrs. Mason, flushed, bewildered, and somewhat terrified, responded after a minute with courage: "If you feel so strongly about it, of course I—but I don't in the least know what to put in that new will."

"We can work something out. I met your cousin to-day—Miss Corinne Hutter."

"Oh; did she drive over?"

"She drove over. Why don't you stick her in as residuary? The last of the family; it's a logical thing to do. Nothing fantastic about that."

Mrs. Mason drew herself up. "Corinne Hutter doesn't wish to be in Syl's and my wills, Henry."

"These family feuds—I know they're tiresome; but you can leave her the money anyway, and she can build libraries with it."

"It would be most unsuitable to leave her all that money. Syl and I shall arrange an annuity in due course," said Mrs. Mason stiffly. "I'm not going to have Corinne get up after we're dead and say she won't have tainted money!"

"Is she likely to?" Gamadge had to smile.

"You don't know the airs she puts on. I think Syl and I are very good to put up with her at all!"

"Well, we must figure out some other deserving residuary

NOTHING CAN RESCUE ME 89

legatee. Oh, look here!" For Mrs. Mason had begun to cry bitterly. "This won't do; what's the matter?"

"I don't know who cares about me enough to deserve it. Even Sally only thinks of Bill; she divorced him, but she still thinks of him, I know she does. Evelyn's the only real friend I have, to leave my money to!"

"Forget about who thinks of you and who doesn't. You're not old enough to bog down in this feeble way, Florence."

"I'm so alone. I can't get about as I used, and Tim leads his own life."

"Do you encourage people to come to you with tales about one another?"

"Of course not!"

"No, but do you? And then do you tackle the culprits?" She began to sob.

"They never tell me anything. They think they can make a fool of me. I must know what's going on, to protect myself."

"But that kind of thing lands you in a perfect hotbed of resentment, and mutual distrust, and bad feeling all round. People don't know who's been telling on them, and they're all ready to flit at one another's throats. Oh, well." He patted her arm. "The thing is to make a sensible will. We'll discuss that later—you can leave the bulk of the money to that Home in Bethea."

"And the Church, Henry."

"SS. Gervase and Protase. Now I'm going down to confer with Syl. We'll have your New York place opened, and Mason shall stay here and look after Underhill. You're clearing out when I do."

"But, Henry!" Flustered, and rather excited, she peered at him tearfully from behind her handkerchief. "Why?"

"Why? Because, my dear girl, you've created such an ammunition dump around you that I'm afraid to leave you in it. Sparks are flying already. We don't want anything more to happen like that business with your book. When you get to New York see your doctor. Or have you one here?"

"Except for my special arthritis régime I have Dr. Burbage, from Bethea. We've had him ever since Father died. He's very good."

"He can recommend a Southern trip. Take Louise. It'll do you worlds of good to travel,"

"I've never been so ordered about in my life!" But Mrs. Mason seemed pleased by Gamadge's brusque methods.

"You need to get away from the lot of them," he said. "You need to stop worrying about who loves you and who doesn't. Now I'll go talk to Syl, and then I'll be back. Don't tell anybody about your plans yet—you want Burbage's orders behind you."

"I don't know how I shall ever get ready by to-morrow. Shout for Louise."

Gamadge went and shouted for Louise, whose room, as he remembered, was just at the head of the back stairs. Then he descended to the first floor; at the door of the library a single note from the old clock within told him that it was half-past three.

He did not go through the library, however; a curious muffled sound like crying drew him along the hall to the cupboard under the stairs. When he arrived at it a scratching prepared him to see the griffons tumble out as soon as he opened the door; they did so, evidently in a vile temper, and dashed past him towards the front of the house.

Mildly surprised, he tapped on the office door, received no answer to his knock, and went in. The room was in semi-darkness as he had left it, and seemed empty; planchette was no longer on the bridge table, and suddenly he caught sight of its little white wheels on the floor, midway between the door and the window. It lay on its back, legs in air, with exactly the helpless look of an over-turned bug or beetle. Gamadge, more and more puzzled, advanced through the dusk.

After a step or two he halted, frozen; Sylvanus lay behind

the bridge table, fallen sidewise, with the little chair across his feet. There was a pool of blood under the frightful wound on his head, and at the edge of the pool lay the weapon that had killed him—a bronze Chinese lady from the library mantelpiece, the one that leaned slightly towards the left.

Gamadge raised his eyes and looked at the open library door. The murderer had come through it after snatching the bronze from the mantle; had dealt that smashing blow from behind. Sylvanus, falling forward, had struck the light table, and planchette had bounded to the floor. When? Gamadge looked over his shoulder into the dark hall, and across to the stair cupboard; some thirty-five minutes earlier he had seen the griffons rush for the back stairs, and Louise had said that they must be hunting Sylvanus. If the murderer had shut them up in their familiar prison to quiet their barking, Sylvanus had perhaps been murdered while Gamadge and Louise conversed in his bedroom.

Gamadge walked around the bridge table and touched Sylvanus's outflung wrist; then, suddenly whirling, he sped out of the office, down the hall, and halfway up the front stairs. But his momentary panic was baseless—he had a glimpse of Louise within the doorway of Mrs. Mason's room, and he heard Florence's voice chattering busily. He came back to the office, closed and locked the doors, and went to the desk telephone.

When he heard the operator's voice he said shortly: "State police."

A few seconds later somebody addressed him in a gruff kind of chant: "State Police Headquarters, Bethea. Sergeant Begg."

"I wish to report a homicide."

Sergeant Begg was not startled: "Those drunks up in the valley again?"

"Drunks? No. Mr. Hutter's been killed; at the Hutter place, above Erasmus."

"For the love of—"

"I'm a guest in the house. I found him about two minutes ago. Back of his head's smashed in, and the weapon's here. Done within the last thirty-five minutes. I'm locking the room—haven't told anybody."

Sergeant Begg said: "For the love of—what's your name?"

"Gamadge. Henry Gamadge, New York."

"Any men on the place for a round-up?"

"Er, I think it was an inside job."

"I'll get hold of the Inspector if I can. Keep an eye on the room till somebody gets there."

Sergeant Begg rang off. Gamadge went back to the bridge table, and looked at the paper which had been under planchette; there was no mark on it except the long, light track which planchette had made when Sylvanus's dying hands first shoved it, before he struck the table and it bounded off to the floor. Gamadge was sure that Sylvanus would not have waited long for a message; certainly not ten minutes—until three o'clock. Had the griffons been shut up before or after the murder? Before it, of course; as soon as they met the murderer in the hall.

Gamadge looked into the stair cupboard, and pulled on its hanging light. A neat cupboard it was now, with the floor clear except for garden tools and baskets under a shelf; a riding-crop and gloves on the shelf, a couple of sou'wester hats and rubber coats on the hooks. One of the gloves was bloodstained, and the thinner and shorter raincoat had blood on its right cuff and low down on its right front, near the hem. These last stains looked as if they had dripped there; from the bronze, perhaps, when the murderer lowered it after the blow; those bronzes had smooth, rounded pedestals—blood would drip from them. Gamadge had seen the pedestal of the one that killed Sylvanus, and observed that its head was clean.

If the griffons had been shut into the cupboard before the

murder, wouldn't they have come rushing out again when the murderer replaced the gloves and the raincoat? They would, unless ordered to stay where they were by someone whom they implicitly obeyed. Thinking this over, Gamadge shut the cupboard door and took up a strategic position at the foot of the stairs; whence he could watch the hall and its doors, and watch the drawing-room; and—most important of all, to him—whence he could hear Louise and Mrs. Mason. Except for them the house was quiet—rather too quiet for his peace. Mason might still be on his walk, Corinne Hutter on hers, but what had become of Susie Burt, of Mrs. Deedes, of Evelyn Wing? Had the latter gone upstairs? He looked into the drawing-room, but it was empty.

Had Percy gone on his walk in the walled garden? It had not quite rained, but while Gamadge was with Mrs. Mason it had begun a sort of drizzle.

Twice Gamadge went all the way up to the second floor, to assure himself that all was well with Florence Mason. The second time Louise almost caught him; she was carrying a griffon along to the hall bathroom and scolding it; blood on its paw, she complained, but she couldn't find that it had hurt itself.

At four minutes past four two motor-cycles and a police car came quietly up the drive; Gamadge, from the front doorway, watched one of the officers station the others; three outside the house, while a fourth and fifth came up the steps. Their superior followed them; a stocky middle-aged, greying man with a long and square chin, a long and blunt nose, a thin mouth and a direct stare. He stopped in front of Gamadge to ask: "You the Mr. Gamadge that called us?"

"Yes. Thought you'd never get here."

"We made pretty good time. I'm Lieutenant Windorp, Inspector of State Police at Bethea. The coroner's on his way. I called the county."

"Glad they got hold of you. This way"

"Stay at the door, Ridley. Come along, Morse. This is Sergeant Morse, Mr. Gamadge. He'll take notes for me."

Gamadge nodded to Sergeant Morse over a shoulder. He unlocked the office door, and for ten minutes did most of the talking. Lieutenant Windorp made an excellent listener, and in fact did little more, after he had pulled back the curtains and raised the blind, than listen to Gamadge and look about the room—at the body of Sylvanus, at planchette recumbent, at the paper on the table, the bronze statuette on the floor. Then he allowed Gamadge, still talking, to show him the cupboard under the stairs. Sergeant Morse, a young man training himself to be completely official, took notes with speed and competence; but he could not prevent his eyes from bulging.

When Gamadge had related, in the minutest detail, everything (except his conversation with Mrs. Mason and his conversation with Louise) that had happened after he had left Sylvanus to planchette, Windorp remarked that he seemed to be a fair witness.

"I've had a little experience. I know the kind of information you people want. By the way—I haven't told you that my poor friend here, and his aunt Mrs. Mason, got me up yesterday on a job."

"Job?"

"You'll be interested, but that story can wait until you have time to listen to it. What I should like to impress upon you now is the condition of Mrs. Mason's alibi."

Windorp, surveying him dispassionately, said: "I know Mrs. Mason fairly well. Didn't know she had a motive for killing her nephew."

"Well, that's just it; you and I are aware that it's absurd to dream of her killing anybody for any reason; but the fact is that Syl's death gives her the free use of the Hutter fortune—about ten millions. Up till now she's only had half the income; Sylvanus had the other half."

Windorp's face did not alter. "His death releases the capital?"

"Yes. But of course she's always known that, and only today she was discussing her will with me—on the basis of her private fortune of about five hundred thousand."

Windorp ran his hand over the top of his head.

"She expected me in her room from lunch-time on," continued Gamadge. "I left Hutter at ten to three, went upstairs with the maid Louise a couple of minutes later, talked to her in my room for a few minutes, and found Mrs. Mason settled on her chaise-longue with a book at three-three. That's what the clock on her mantel said. I was with her until just on three-thirty, when I went down and found Hutter. She had less than ten minutes to shut up the dogs, commit the murder, get the raincoat on and off, and dodge up to her room again; knowing I was due any minute. It's out of the question. I wish you'd let me break Syl's death to her, lieutenant. It'll be a frightful shock. And somebody's sure to see those troops of yours any minute now."

Windorp reflected. At last he said: "Tell you what we'll do. That man of theirs, Thomas; I've seen him around in Bethea for years. Tell him to get Mrs. Mason down here."

"Thanks. In the drawing-room? You'll want the library clear."

"And you don't want her as close to the scene of action as that. All right," said Windorp imperturbably, "the drawing-room."

Gamadge rang the bell beside the swing door. Thomas appeared, looking stupefied; he had caught a glimpse of the troopers, and now, at sight of Windorp, showed agitation.

"There's been some trouble, Tom," said Gamadge, "and Lieutenant Windorp wants to talk to Mrs. Mason. Don't say trouble—just ask her to step down and see him—and me."

"Yes, sir. Might I ask what—"

"No, because if you know what, Mrs. Mason will get it out of you." He added: "When she's down, stand by in the dining-room with brandy."

Thomas went up the back stairs. Gamadge and Windorp retired to the drawing-room, where Gamadge supplied the lieutenant with additional detail until Mrs. Mason came down. She was alert and inquisitive, but not alarmed.

"Well, I'm delighted to see you, Lieutenant Windorp, but I don't know why you're here, because none of the cars is out. We hardly ever use them. Don't tell me any of the men has been doing anything? They're never in trouble!"

Windorp discreetly permitted Gamadge to break the news; called Thomas in when she collapsed; helped him to administer brandy; and when she revived, permitted Gamadge to take her up to her room.

CHAPTER NINE

Defence Programme

ANOTHER CAR, AND THEN ANOTHER, drove up to the front door; there was commotion in the hall, a rush of footsteps, a slamming of doors. The house was astir by the time that Gamadge and Mrs. Mason had reached her room.

Mrs. Deedes came up behind them, gasping. "Henry, what is it? There are police on the grounds, and a man with a badge in the lower hall, and a man with a bag—he looks like a doctor. What has happened?"

Gamadge said: "Help me to get her on her bed." Mrs. Deedes, with a wild glance at him, put her arm around her friend. Mrs. Mason was laid tenderly on the left-hand bed, and supported by a multitude of little pink and blue pillows; Mrs. Deedes drew the eiderdown up over her feet. She opened her eyes.

"Syl's dead," she whispered. "Somebody killed him."

Mrs. Deedes raised a shocked face to Gamadge, who nodded. "It's true, Sally. Ring her doctor."

She went to the telephone, which stood on a table beside the fireplace. As she lifted it, Gamadge said: "Tell him to bring two nurses."

"Two?" she faltered.

"Two. She's not to be alone day or night until she can be moved from Underhill."

"Alone, Henry? We wouldn't leave her alone!"

"I want two nurses."

At the look in his eyes she turned away, and began to talk into the mouthpiece. Evelyn Wing appeared at the door.

"Evvie!" Mrs. Mason held out her arms. Miss Wing, without a look at Gamadge, came and bent over the pathetic figure on the bed.

"Evvie, Syl's dead! Somebody killed him!"

"I know. A policeman came and told me just now. I must go down. I had to speak to you first."

"Can't you stay with me?" Mrs. Mason clutched her.

"Dear Mrs. Mason, we all have to go and talk to the officer—Lieutenant Windorp."

"He's so nice; you'll like him. Does he say it was those awful people up in the valley? They used to be bootleggers, and kidnap people."

"I don't know what he thinks." Even now Miss Wing did not look at Gamadge. She said: "Of course they're asking us all questions."

"I don't know why they should ask *you* questions."

"They want to know whether we heard anything."

"Oh, Evvie, I can't realize it!"

"No, of course not. Dear Mrs. Mason, I must go. There's a man waiting."

"I'll stay," said Gamadge. "I won't leave you until the doctor and the nurses come."

Miss Wing straightened, and her eyes met Gamadge's at last. "Nurses?"

"Mrs. Mason has had a great shock."

"I could nurse her."

"In a case like this one's time isn't one's own. Better rely on professionals."

Mrs. Deedes came from the telephone. She was white and shaken, but she spoke cheerfully to her friend: "Dr. Burbage was at home; isn't that lucky? And he says he can get hold of Miss Mudge. You like Miss Mudge, Florrie."

"She's very nice." Mrs. Mason, a volatile type, was recovering; she had relaxed on her pillows, and a faint flush was growing on her cheek-bones. Sylvanus's death had of course shocked her greatly, but she would not grieve for him; their affection had never been deep.

Sergeant Morse appeared in the doorway. "Lieutenant would like you ladies to come down right away and wait in the dining-room.

"Go down, both of you," said Mrs. Mason, bravely. "Go right down. You must do everything you can to help Windorp catch the man. Henry will take care of me."

Gamadge consulted Sergeant Morse with a glance, and the sergeant's nod permitted him to stay. He waited until Miss Wing and Mrs. Deedes had been shepherded from the room; then he closed the hall door and the door into the bath, and came to sit down beside the bed. "Now," he said, smiling, but looking determined.

"'Now,' Henry? What do you mean?"

"Now we must think fast. What a comfort it is to deal with a woman of affairs; a woman like you, who can throw off shock, and pull herself together, and face the immediate future."

"Oh dear; I can't—yet."

"Now is the time for action; you can relax when the nurses come, and stop thinking completely. Here—let me plump up those pillows for you—you'll feel much stronger sitting up. I know you, Florrie; no fans and aspirin for you; you need a cigarette."

He got her almost upright against her cushions, lighted a cigarette for her, and one for himself. "Now," he said, "we're all set. Poor Syl is dead, and you are a multi-millionaire—with the free disposal of your father's fortune."

Mrs. Mason's flush deepened; she gazed at him, startled and greatly excited. "Henry—I never thought!"

"Of course you didn't."

"I never dreamed I should outlive poor Syl! I simply can't realize it at all!"

"As your adviser I must remind you that you must make that new will—make it without a moment's loss of time."

Mrs. Mason looked staggered. "Make it *now*?"

"Of course. We talked that over. It mustn't stand as it is—not a day."

"Yes, but, Henry, there can't be any such hurry as that! I'm not going to die, you know"

"You certainly are not." Gamadge, looking at her, marvelled at the defence mechanisms of the human brain.

"And I do think it's most inconsiderate of you to badger me like this at such a time," she protested.

"Best thing in the world for you; anybody will tell you so."

"You men would make us talk business in an earthquake. Oh, have it your own way," said Mrs. Mason, in a weak voice.

"Fine. Where's that will you made on Thursday?"

"In the desk, somewhere. One of the drawers."

He rummaged until he found it—a neat job, folded lengthwise, and inscribed: *Last Will and Testament of Florence Hutter Mason*. He collected a blotting-pad, paper, and a fountain pen, brought them and the will to her, and placed the blotter on her knees. Then, getting out his own pen, he sat down.

"Now," he said, "let's see. The important thing is to dispose of the residuary estate."

"I've been thinking that over," she said briskly. "I'm going to leave it in equal shares to the Bethea Home for Destitute Children and the church I told you about in New York."

"Good. Very sensible."

"It's wonderful to be able to do such useful things."

"Isn't it? Now for the other bequests."

"I think I might double Sally's and Susie Burt's."

"A hundred thousand apiece? Very nice."

"And a hundred thousand to Evelyn Wing," said Mrs. Mason firmly, "and my personal chattels, and Underhill."

Gamadge, making no comment, wrote it down. "What are you doing for Mason?" he asked.

She pressed her lips together.

"Now, Florrie; I know you think he wrote those things into your book and tried to get rid of Miss Wing, and I know he took Susie Burt to a night club; but you have no more proof against him, after all, when it comes to the business of tampering with your script, than you have against the others; and you're leaving them a lot of money. This will can be changed later; but if you should die suddenly, having cut him out, he'd put up an awful fight."

"I don't believe he could break my will."

"He'd do his best."

"Well, then, I'll say a hundred thousand—but it's provisional."

Gamadge said gravely: "All these bequests are provisional. Now, what about something for Corinne Hutter?"

Mrs. Mason's face assumed the look of mulish obstinacy that it took on whenever Corinne Hutter's financial affairs were mentioned. "I told you I don't wish her to get up and say she's too good for Hutter money!"

"She won't."

"She refused the annuity Syl and I offered her."

"Put her down anyway. People will talk if you don't; they'll say you were mean. Let her say what she likes—everybody will think she's making a perfect fool of herself."

"Well; Syl and I thought of five hundred a year."

"Then it ought to be a thousand, now, since you're doubling the other bequests." Gamadge jotted it down; Mrs. Mason, watching him with some annoyance, tapped the blotting-pad with the end of her fountain pen.

"Servants," said Gamadge.

"I'll leave them as they were. Syl and I arranged that between us. They're in his will, too," Mrs. Mason's face clouded, and her eyes filled with tears. "I simply can't realize that he's gone first! And such a dreadful way—oh, Henry, who *could* have done such a thing?"

"Windorp will find out. Now just a minute more, Florrie. Executors."

"The bank's one, and poor Syl was the other."

"Let me put Bob Macloud down. He knows Syl's affairs, and your affairs, and he's incorruptible, and he'll approve of this will. I want you to let me call him up for you now. He ought to come out as soon as he can get here."

"He charges so much."

"You can afford to pay him anything. Let me get hold of him for you. You'll need him."

"Oh, very well. Whom shall we get to witness this will, Henry?"

"Couple of State police—how's that for law?" He laid his notes on the blotter. "Now just you copy these out, and here's the other will to go by. You're an old hand at it—you'll know what to do."

Mrs. Mason, reading his notes, slowly unscrewed the top of her fountain pen. After a moment she looked up at Gamadge; her high colour was fading, and her eyes were frightened.

"Henry?"

"Yes."

"Henry—could one of *them* have killed him?"

"One of them?"

"Oh, it isn't possible!"

Gamadge thought: Got it at last. He asked: "Why should any of them kill Sylvanus, Florence?"

"Because"—she looked at him, and then down at the rough draft of the will, confusion and horror in her round eyes—"because he knew who put those things in my book!"

No, she couldn't imagine herself in danger from her friends; by some fortunate lapse of intelligence she was not as yet worrying on her own account. But she was sufficiently dismayed by her ingenious theory, and repeated it in another form: "He was going to tell, and they killed him so that he couldn't!"

"It's possible."

"And you've let me leave all of them all this money!"

"They can't every one of them have killed him, Florence; and I don't believe the guilty party will ever inherit under this will, or any will of yours. You'll make dozens more, you know," he said, smiling a little.

"Why won't he inherit?"

"Because let's hope that he—or she—will be discovered."

Mrs. Mason, her terrified eyes on his, stammered: "You made me cut Evelyn's legacy down; Evelyn would *never*—"

"She has friends, you know; they all have friends or backers."

"I simply don't believe any of them did it! I can't! It must have been one of those creatures in the valley that keep on marrying their own nieces."

"Let me do the worrying. You write out that will."

She slowly applied herself to the task. Gamadge went to the telephone, tracked Macloud to his club, and communicated the news of Sylvanus's death in a couple of dead languages. Macloud, after a long pause, replied incredulously and in consternation:

"Do I understand that *notre ami archéologique a été tué avec un objet d'art?*"

"That's right."

"Great Heavens."

"Florence wants you up here as soon as you can make it; you're her lawyer again."

"Tell him to stay over Sunday," called Mrs. Mason.

Macloud replied to the invitation by saying that he would drive up in time for a late dinner, but that he would have to return to town on Sunday afternoon. "It's ten after five," he said. "I'll pack a bag and get my car. Perhaps I'd better have dinner on the way."

Gamadge consulted Mrs. Mason, who said that she would order dinner for half-past eight.

"How is she?" asked Macloud.

"Behaving splendidly. She is at present making testamentary dispositions."

"What! Again?"

"At my urgent request."

Macloud, after a pause, said he was glad of it. Then he rang off, and Gamadge crossed to the long window nearest him. He opened one of its doors, and stepped out on a little iron balcony.

The western mountain ranges and the nearer hilltops had disappeared in mist; mist was beginning to shroud the line of beeches that concealed the stream and cut the sloping grounds of Underhill from its meadows. The stream had a muted tone; not its most cheerful voice by any means, thought Gamadge, as he leaned on the railing to look downwards.

Immediately below him were the dining-room windows, which gave on a stretch of lawn. To the left, beyond a bricked walk, a tall yew hedge enclosed the kitchen premises and drying-ground; farther down, a double hedge of yew curved south and west; it was the approach to the walled garden. The back steps of the house were occupied by a State policeman whom Gamadge had already seen, and had heard addressed by Windorp as Ridley.

"Hi," said Gamadge; adding, as the officer looked up, "Mrs. Mason wants you and another man to come up here for a minute."

The trooper got to his feet. "Mrs. Mason wants two officers?"

"Tell Lieutenant Windorp she wants you to witness her will."

Ridley, somewhat bewildered, opened the back door and raised his voice. At his summons a man in plain clothes came out, looked up at Gamadge, and then settled down on the steps. Ridley disappeared. Five minutes later he and another trooper were admitted to Mrs. Mason's room, and received by her with a cry of pleasure:

"Why, Johnny Ridley! And isn't that Officer Beaver?"

Ridley came over to the bed to shake hands; Officer Beaver, a huge youth, said shyly: "I'm awful sorry about Mr. Hutter, ma'am."

"Isn't it dreadful? Your mother will feel so badly, Johnny; she was so fond of poor Syl."

"She'll feel terrible. Hope we get the feller that did it."

"As you see, I have to carry on; there's so much to attend to, and only me to do it. Now that Syl is dead I must make a new will, but all my friends are down for legacies, so they can't be witnesses. And all the servants are in my will, too." She looked suddenly at Gamadge. "But why can't you be a witness, Henry?"

"Think I'll just stay on the sidelines."

"Well, anyway, here it is." Mrs. Mason undoubtedly liked to make wills, and knew all about the formalities of signing and witnessing them. She said: "Now I'm signing; you'd better come and watch me do it."

Officer Ridley leaned over to watch the procedure from the left side of the twin bed; Officer Beaver edged himself between it and the other one; a sense of deep responsibility furrowed his brow.

"Now you're to sign," said Mrs. Mason, handing Ridley her fountain pen.

Ridley signed, Beaver made heavy work of signing, and Gamadge blotted their signatures, folded the will, and bestowed it in a breast pocket. "Till Macloud gets here," he said. "And not a word to anybody, you two; understand?"

"Not a single word," said Mrs. Mason.

"I only hope we catch the feller that killed Mr. Hutter," rumbled Beaver.

"I hope it's one of those men up in the valley." Mrs. Mason's face lost its brightness. She pushed the blotting-pad away and leaned back against her pillows, her head averted and her eyes closed. She looked desolate and old. Gamadge went with the troopers to the door. As they reached it, a handsome, white-moustached man, carrying a black bag and still wearing his over-coat, brushed past them into the room.

CHAPTER TEN

All Nice Folks

"**H**AL BURBAGE!" CRIED Mrs. Mason, sitting up.
"And your friend Miss Mudge. We were lucky to get hold
of her." Dr. Burbage was closely followed by a capped and bon-
neted nurse, carrying a suit-case; Gamadge hurried forward and
took it from her, to be rewarded by a bright smile. Burbage, after
a sharp glance at him, went to his patient.

"Well, Florrie." He put his fingers around her wrist.
"Considering what you've been through in the last hour, you're
doing pretty well. I'm pleased with you."

Mrs. Mason had again become limp and tearful. "Oh, Hal,
it's all too dreadful. I suppose I must have collapsed at first, since
Mr. Gamadge would insist on my having two nurses."

Burbage sat down, put his bag on the floor, and dragged his
coat off. He was about to hang it on the back of his chair, but
Miss Mudge quickly advanced and took it away. "You the man
that wanted two nurses, are you?" he pierced Gamadge with an-

other sharp look. "From the way Mrs. Deedes talked over the telephone I thought you must be a specialist, and I was called in for a consultation."

"I simply have no manners," wailed Mrs. Mason, "Let me introduce you."

"Don't think it's necessary," said Burbage, considering the blunt-featured young man with the greenish eyes. "I'll have a word with Mr. Gamadge after I've settled you, Florrie; or rather, while Miss Mudge is settling you. We'll go outside and she'll put you to bed. I'm going to give you a good once-over, now I'm here. How's the novel getting along?"

"Don't talk about it!"

Burbage, surprised at her vehemence, said: "Mustn't let it lick you. Mustn't let this trouble lick you. I've known you a long time, and never saw anything or anybody lick you yet. You just turn yourself over to Miss Mudge; remember how she got you through the flu last year?"

The smiling Miss Mudge came forward, and Burbage rose. Outside the closed bedroom door he faced Gamadge:

"There's another nurse on the way. What's the idea, young feller?"

"I thought day and night professional nursing was the thing for Mrs. Mason just now. Until Sylvanus's murder has been cleared up."

Burbage knitted his brows. "Windorp's been checking up on you. He had the darnedest rigmarole. The New York City Police Department has their summer camp not so far from this, and Windorp knows some of 'em. He's been telephoning."

Gamadge smiled.

"Says you were good enough to explain that Florence Mason didn't kill Sylvanus Hutter. Florence!"

"I hoped he'd waste no time on Florence. She mustn't be alone, Doctor, or eat or drink a thing the nurses haven't prepared for her: I'm hoping to get her to New York tomorrow. Think she can make it?"

Burbage looked at him, frowning heavily. At last he said:

"Good Lord, I know these people."

"Just at the moment, would you take a chance on them? Syl's death has released the Hutter fortune, and every soul in the house is down for something in her will, and they all know it except Corinne Hutter, whose annuity I made Florence shove in above half an hour ago."

"I suppose it couldn't be those thugs up the valley?"

"Thugs up the valley, Doctor? Chinese bronze used as weapon, front door locked, raincoat and gloves found and put on, office desk undisturbed—"

"I was hoping they'd been scared off." Burbage chewed his lower lip. "I know how it looks. I'll have Florence in shape to go back to New York to-morrow. Windorp's a sensible man; he won't object."

"I thought perhaps you'd get hold of her New York doctor and see if he'd put her in a comfortable rest cure for the time being. Where she'd enjoy herself. Get her away from these people—all of them."

"Good idea; I know the very place, she's been there before." He cast a glance of sombre inquiry at Gamadge. "Mason—if he's not consulted he'll make a row."

"Windorp must handle him."

"Well; I'll give instructions about the food and the nursing. Trust Mudge and Boylan—that's the other one. Windorp seems to think you may be able to give him a hand with this murder. Says you had everything cut and dried for him."

"I had a dead body for him. I had everything cut and dried for the murder; room darkened, all the rest of it. Syl got me up here to look after Florence, and he's dead. I'm not going to let anything happen to Florence Mason."

Miss Mudge put her head around the door to say that Mrs.

Mason was ready for the doctor. Burbage muttered: "See you again," and hurried into the bedroom. Gamadge was turning away, when a voice addressed him from the head of the back stairs: "For goodness' sake, Mr. Gamadge, what is all this, anyhow?"

Gamadge swung about to look up at Miss Corinne Hutter. "Good Heavens," he said, "didn't Windorp get you?"

"Who's Windorp? What's happened? I sat down to finish that tear in the window curtain, and I looked out and saw State police in the yard."

"I gave him your name with the rest. Why didn't they find you? Where on earth have you been?"

"Up here, having a nap after my walk. Where should I be?"

"What time did you get back?"

"Around a quarter past three. I've had a sleep."

"Slept right through it all. Look here, I'm coming up." Again he climbed the dark stairs, and again followed her into the little south-west room. She stood gazing at him, thimble on finger, needle and spool in her hand, amazement growing in her round eyes. He took note of the fact that the bed was against the partition wall, out of sight behind the half-open door.

"Funny the troopers didn't look right into all the rooms," he said. "Somebody'll get a wigging."

"Why?"

"Because there just might have been a strange murderer in the house. Your cousin Sylvanus is dead, Miss Hutter."

"Dead?"

"He was killed. Somebody smashed his head in with one of those bronzes from the library mantelpiece. It happened between ten minutes to three and half-past, and you just missed seeing the murderer."

Miss Hutter justified his opinion of her Roman quality; she looked at him in silence, and then sat down in her rocking chair. After a pause she remarked: "I can't take it in."

Gamadge also sat down. "Don't blame you," he said.

"Where was he when he was killed?"

"In the office, working planchette."

"Where was everybody?"

"Don't know. I found him, and didn't see a soul except Louise and Mrs. Mason. They're out of it, anyway."

She pondered this. Then she said: "Anybody could get in, you know. They don't lock the back door much in the day-time; it was unlocked when I came back. The servants wouldn't see the person come in unless one of them happened to be in the hall or the passage."

Gamadge told the story of the raincoat and the griffons. As he finished it the griffons trotted into the room, and he pointed to the second in line. "That fellow had blood on his paw, afterwards. I think he got it when the murderer hung the raincoat up in the closet."

Miss Hutter looked faintly nauseated, but said calmly:

"It's a girl, Dodo. Bobo's the boy."

'Whose dogs are they?"

"Cousin Florence's, but they like Cousin Tim Mason the best." She added, rather quickly, "They like lots of people."

"Now, look here, Miss Hutter." Gamadge leaned forward, his eyes on hers. "I want you to forget everything—everything except the fact that your cousin Sylvanus was brutally killed. I don't think there's much doubt that he was killed by an inmate of this house. I want you to be frank with me, and discuss the potentialities for murder of all these people."

She reached out to pick up the corner of the muslin curtain, studied the half-mended rent in it, and slowly began to sew the remaining gap together. Then she said:

"They're all nice folks."

"How nice? Is Miss Burt as nice as Mrs. Deedes, is Percy as nice as Mason? What do you mean by nice, Miss Hutter?"

"I mean they all come from nice families. It would take a good deal to make any of them kill a person."

"It would; what, for instance? Florence suggests that Sylvanus knew who put those extracts into her book, and was killed because he intended to tell; tell me, I suppose. He showed no sign of being about to tell me anything."

"He was quite close-mouthed."

"He was, and he hated a row. But I had stirred him up, and perhaps he was going to reveal something. Perhaps he knew that Miss Burt's affair with Mason was more serious than Florence supposed."

"Susie Burt wouldn't have a serious affair with anybody unless the person had money."

"Now we come to it. Nobody in the outfit had money but Sylvanus and Florence; now she has it all."

Miss Hutter's spool rolled from her lap to the floor, but she retrieved it before Gamadge could do so. When she sat up again there was a slight flush on her face. She said: "Terrible."

"So terrible that I have got two nurses for Florence."

"I'm glad of it."

"Thank goodness you don't protest, and talk about thugs up the valley."

"Well, I did talk about somebody from outside."

"Before you knew the facts."

"I don't know many facts yet. Would Cousin Tim Mason get a good deal of money if Cousin Florence died?"

"A good deal; less than he was down for at one time."

"I don't mean that Cousin Tim would do these things. I was thinking of Susie, and it's kind of mean of me."

"We must think of these things. Miss Burt is down for something too. It would be worth while, I suppose."

"I don't see what else Cousin Sylvanus could have been going to tell, if that's what he was killed for," said Corinne, rocking.

"Well, perhaps he was killed just to release the money to Florence."

"Mrs. Deedes wouldn't kill him, or Cousin Florence, or anybody."

"Not even for Bill Deedes?"

Corinne slowly shook her head. "Of course I don't know, but I should say not. She isn't the kind."

"Miss Wing?"

Corinne shook her head. "She isn't the kind either."

"She's down for a whacking legacy, you know; we can't tell who's been snooping about and reading drafts or copies of Florence's wills."

"I can't see Evelyn Wing committing murder."

"Remains Mr. Percy; the charming, the accomplished; the serious reader. He seems to have developed a certain interest in Miss Wing, although more or less the property—by report—of Miss Burt. Would you say that *he* could be seriously in love unless there was money in it for him?"

"I guess anybody could be seriously in love without there being money in it; but I don't believe he'd marry without it, any more than Susie Burt would."

"What do you think of him otherwise?"

She snapped off her thread, put the needle and spool carefully into her little sewing-case, and tied the case up. She laid it on the table, and then, slowly tapping her thimbled finger on the table edge, seemed lost in thought. At last she looked at Gamadge. "Are you going to repeat what I say to the police?" she asked.

"I won't repeat an unnecessary word to them."

"If I had to have an enemy, I'd rather have almost anybody but Glen Percy."

"No, really?" Gamadge was much interested. "Would you indeed?"

"Yes, I would."

"Why?"

"When I drove over a couple of weeks ago I went down to

that garden with the walls and the yew hedges. He was by the pool with Susie Burt, and they were talking, and I saw his face."

"Not so beautiful as it usually is?"

"It wasn't beautiful at all. He was talking about Cousin Tim. Then I came around the hedge, and they saw me, and he was pleasant again."

Gamadge was thoughtful. "He seems pleasant enough to Miss Burt now, if a trifle condescending."

"That's just it."

"You're making him out a very queer character indeed."

"I'm not making him out anything."

"If he was reproaching Susie Burt for her affair with Mason, in spite of the fact that he wouldn't marry her unless she had money—oh, look here?"

Corinne looked at him, silent.

"He works out a scheme to do away with your cousin Florence, and marry Miss Burt on the strength of her legacy; which he presumably knows all about. Miss Burt, however, falls in love with Mason; so Percy adapts the plan to Miss Wing. Tampers with the novel, secretly explains to Florence that somebody's trying to get rid of Wing, gets her legacy boosted, and begins to lay siege to her affections. Dear me. No wonder, if that's true, Miss Burt was unable to contain herself when she saw his pretended change of heart. He's beginning to sound like somebody out of an Elizabethan drama himself—'Glenido, a Roman Gentleman.'"

"The only person I ever saw that had his looks," said Corinne Hutter, rather dreamily, "was an Italian on a boat."

"An Italian—on a boat?"

"His baggage was marked for Washington," said Corinne. "It was a ferry boat, and I followed him quite a way up the dock. Perhaps he was a prince; I couldn't describe him."

"I've seen 'em; I know what you mean."

"Well, anyway, you're going to look out for Cousin Florence."

"I most certainly am. And I'm hoping to get her out of here to-morrow."

Officer Ridley passed the door, stopped, retraced his steps, and peered in. Astonishment overspread his face. Gamadge rose, smiling.

"Officer," he said, "meet Miss Hutter."

"I know Johnny Ridley," said Corinne drily.

"Good gosh. Lieutenant read me the names you gave him, Mr. Gamadge, and I wrote 'em down. When he said Miss Hutter I thought he meant Mrs. Mason; lots of people around here still call her Miss Hutter. Was you in this room all the time, Corinne?"

"Yes, I was. You better go down," said Corinne "and tell them I was overlooked in the excitement."

"You ought to be in the dining-room," muttered Ridley.

"I guess I can take my time about it. You did." She rose. "Any chance of my getting back to Erasmus for supper?"

Gamadge and Ridley exchanged a glance. Gamadge said:

"None. I should say that you would be here all night."

"Then somebody'll have to lend me a nightgown. Can't one of you boys drive down to Erasmus and buy me a toothbrush?"

Office Ridley had recovered his official tone: "You will please go down to the dining-room, wait there, and see Lieutenant Windorp in the library. Then you go to the parlour where the others are."

"Trouble is, I'm getting hungry."

"They re having a big tea."

She raised her hands to do her hair, skewered back a wisp or so, and walked out of the room.

Ridley asked with annoyance: "Where in time was she all afternoon?"

"Out for a walk, and then having a nap."

"She's just the way she used to be when she gave us books out of the library." He went on, leading the way down the back stairs and switching lights on at every switch he came to: "The body's been taken to Bethea, and they've locked up the office. We got a matron from the Bethea jail, but she can't find any bloodstains on any of the women's clothes. She'll have to go over Corinne Hutter."

"Corinne Hutter will love that."

"The servants are out of it, anyhow. The indoor ones were together out back and there weren't any men on the place to-day, as it's Saturday, except a groom and a boy. They were together in the stables. Mr. Mason finally got home. Say, Mr. Gamadge, these are nice folks; did one of 'em go crazy?"

"There are so many ways of going crazy, Officer."

They went down to the first floor, Ridley turning on light switches all the way.

CHAPTER ELEVEN

Percy Rejects an Alibi

WHEN GAMADGE ENTERED the drawing-room he found Mason, highball glass in hand, walking back and forth as if for a wager; while Percy, ensconced behind a colossal silver tray, poured himself a cup of tea. As Gamadge approached the sofa Percy uncovered a muffin dish and offered it to him.

"It makes me hungry to be grilled," he said. "How about you? Or haven't you been grilled yet?"

"I've been grilled." Gamadge sat down beside him.

Mason stopped in the middle of the room. "What's all this about my not being allowed to see Florence?" he demanded in a loud voice.

Gamadge, teapot in hand, looked up at him. "I suppose the nurse won't let her see anybody."

"I ought to be with her at a time like this. I shall insist on being with her. Nurse? She has two nurses. Aren't there enough women in the house now without getting in two nurses?"

Percy murmured: "He doesn't use his head."

"Use my head? What do you mean?" Mason glared at him. "If somebody in the house has gone crazy and started swinging at us, a man's better protection for Florence than a trained nurse is." He drained his glass. "Sally's the only person around here who ever seemed crazy to me," he went on, "and I don't think she's crazy enough to kill anybody.

Percy remarked to his teacup: "They say you can go mad without knowing it; an eerie notion, and one I never believed in. If I were going mad, I'm sure I should have a nagging suspicion that something was wrong."

Mason stopped beside a console near the doorway to pour whisky into his glass from a decanter. He said: "I don't know what's got into Windorp. I came home from my walk, and the trooper hustled me into the library without telling me a word of what had happened; naturally I refused to answer questions. When I did explain that I'd simply been for my usual hike upstream, you'd have thought by the way Windorp looked at me that people hadn't the use of their legs. I'm a walker, always was." He swallowed the neat whisky in his tumbler at a gulp.

Percy glanced at him over his shoulder. He said: "You need food, not whisky. I understand how you feel, though; it's a jolt to find oneself being ordered about for the first time since school."

"Whatever I need," replied Mason, "I don't need advice from you—or sympathy, either."

Percy said, with a faintly humorous look at Gamadge, "Few tears are being shed for poor Sylvanus Hutter. The truth is, one hardly knew him; he was so utterly absorbed in himself and his hobbies that one couldn't get near him at all. I often think that persons who care exclusively for the inanimate become only half animate themselves." He added with some annoyance, as Mason resumed his restless pacing: "I don't know why you should be in this state, I'm sure. If you have no alibi, neither has any of the rest of us."

"Alibi?" Mason stood rigid to glare at him. "What do you mean? By this time Windorp knows that I left the house before half-past two and never got back until half-past four."

"We certainly did hear the door slam." Percy refilled his teacup.

Mason, inarticulate, opened and shut his mouth. Gamadge looked inquiringly at Percy, who responded with a smile. "Merely the retort courteous," he explained. "Mason has been reminding me that it's common knowledge I said I was going for a walk myself in the walled garden. He also reminds me that people can go in and out of the house by the back door without being seen. He doesn't quite understand that the second fact is in the nature of a boomerang."

"I didn't say you said you were going for a walk in the walled garden," snapped Mason. "I said you did go there. Miss Wing saw you there."

"She is mistaken," said Percy with serenity. "It began to drizzle, so instead of going out I went up to my room, where I read and dozed until summoned by a cop."

"She was there herself, so she says," insisted Mason, "from about a quarter to three until about five after. She saw you in the place just before she left."

"She is mistaken."

"Or making it all up?" suggested Mason, with a mirthless smile. "Perhaps she thinks you might give each other an alibi."

"If she says she was there and saw somebody, she was there and saw somebody; but not me."

"And it's not much of an alibi," said Gamadge. "Syl's murderer could have got down there by three, or I'm much mistaken. But why should Syl's murderer have gone there? And does Miss Wing think that this fetch of Mr. Percy's saw *her*?"

"I don't know," said Mason, "but he needn't have. The place is a perfect maze—you can dodge in and out around the hedges."

"I don't know what my ghost did," said Percy in a languid voice, slightly muted by muffin. "They haven't confronted Miss Wing with me yet."

Gamadge asked: "Is this garden a well-known beauty spot? Is it frequented by tourists?"

"Tourists?" shouted Mason. "Tourists? There's only one way into the place—the Yew Walk; unless you want to climb an eight-foot brick wall."

"Yew," murmured Percy. "It's an American variety, but I always said, and I still say, that it isn't the thing to use here; we have plenty of native stuff for hedges. Of course yew is effective against brick, under a bright sky."

Gamadge was leaning back with half-closed eyes. Presently he opened them to inquire of Percy: "Do you usually keep your hat and coat in the cupboard under the stairs?"

Percy hunched his shoulders together as if shrinking from a physical blow. "Spare me the stair cupboard," he implored. "I refuse to be reminded of the stair cupboard. No, it held only that fatal raincoat of Hutter's, and one of Mason's. My hat and topcoat are with the other hats and coats, in the new hall closet. Why?"

Mrs. Deedes came into the room. "Tim," she said, "I think you might try to see Florence now. They let me have tea with her. But those nurses hover like bats." Mason swung from the room, and she came to sit down on the sofa in the place vacated for her by Percy. "Don't disturb yourselves, children," she said wearily. "Oh, how I wish we could all go to bed until this is all over. They won't let us have one moment's peace."

"Let's hope they'll find that it was one of those Jukes up the valley after all," said Percy, making himself comfortable in another chair.

"Oh, it wasn't." She turned a drawn and anxious face to him. "I know it wasn't, and I blame myself very much. I didn't know that poor little Syl was going to use planchette; I would have

warned him. There have been mischievous influences in the
house for a good while, and this afternoon a really evil spirit got
through."

"Why," asked Percy, in a tone of inexhaustible patience,
"should an evil spirit have attacked and killed Sylvanus Hutter, of
all people, with a Chinese bronze?"

"Have you seen those African images in his room, Glen?"

"Yes; ancient sorcery, and very interesting."

"They're evil—really evil. Sylvanus treated forbidden things
without respect, and they have turned upon him."

Percy, after a moment of staring silence, remarked that he
didn't think the African images called for respect.

"One respects the awful," said Mrs. Deedes, "wherever…"

Susie Burt came into the room, looking, Gamadge thought,
like a piece of Florentine enamel in her sapphire sports dress.
Her blue eyes were stony, her features rigid as if cut from stone.
She walked directly to the bell beside the dining-room door, and
pushed it. Thomas came wavering in, pale and vague.

"I'd like a Martini, Thomas," she said in a cold voice.

"Very well, Miss." He wavered away.

"Poor Thomas," said Percy, "it's sporting of him to struggle
on with his work. Couldn't you have waited a couple of hours for
that drink, Susie, or mixed it yourself?"

"No, I couldn't." She sat down on the bench in front of the
grand piano; an immense instrument, which filled the south-
west corner of the room.

Percy, raising his eyebrows, inquired: "Has Lieutenant
Windorp been vexing you? Was he annoyed because you also
were reading and dozing in your room while Hutter was being
murdered? He must be used to the statement by this time. Were
you reading and dozing, Mrs. Deedes?"

"I was resting. I wasn't dozing."

"Corinne Hutter was," said Gamadge.

Percy said with a smile: "I didn't know Corinne was on the

premises. Has she still the anchorite complex, I wonder? All very well, but so many of them seem to have ended up on all fours."

Mrs. Deedes asked: "Did you go out, Glen? It seems that Evelyn did, and Lieutenant Windorp was very anxious to know whether you did; I couldn't tell him."

"I didn't go out, but my astral body appears to have taken a stroll in the garden."

"Somebody's been telling Lieutenant Windorp a lot of things about us all." Mrs. Deedes frowned. "He kept asking me the queerest questions. I didn't know what he was getting at."

Susie Burt said; "Yes, he heard stuff about me, too; so I told him things about the rest of you." She looked at Percy, a straight, cold look. "I told him you'd been reading every one of those books."

"What books?" he inquired mildly.

"Those books that somebody took quotations from to put in Mrs. Mason's novel. Every night it happened, you left the book out. I saw it after you went up to bed. I remember perfectly well."

"I remember perfectly well, too; and I remember that by next morning the books were put away."

Gamadge said: "But you didn't distress Mrs. Mason by telling her that the perilous stuff was coming from her own library."

"No, I didn't."

Susie said: "I didn't know the quotations came out of those books, but I do now; I've known ever since Mr. Gamadge said what books they were. I wasn't going to tell, but if people are telling things about me I'll tell things about them."

"This murder," said Percy, "is having serious repercussions on our characters."

"I told Lieutenant Windorp that Mr. Deedes is in Mrs. Deedes's apartment in New York right now," continued Susie. "Living there."

Sally looked at her in silence.

"Mrs. Mason sent me around to see how your cold was getting on," Susie told her, "and the doorman let me go up, and the door was ajar, and Mr. Deedes was in there—asleep. I didn't tell Mrs. Mason, but she might as well know it now."

"Windorp must be dizzy with all this free information," said Percy.

"He thinks I'm a splendid witness."

"Well—that isn't quite the word for it; not in police circles." He looked at her through his lashes. She was about to reply, thought better of it, got up from the piano bench and went out through the dining-room into the back hall.

"It's tough, Mrs. Deedes," said Percy, after a pause. "Very tough."

"I had to take Bill in," she answered drearily. "He's been ill, and that woman he was going to marry let him down. Florence won't understand. She'll be so angry—so horrified."

"I bet Louise spilled the Mason-Susie stuff to Windorp," said Percy. "She has her knife into Susie, and she'd want to explain that Mason was a dear, sweet fellow and a victim, and wouldn't hurt a fly. I hope she won't start on me; it'll be the ruin of me."

"She'll tell him charming things," said Gamadge. "She's told 'em to me."

"Oh, God."

Sergeant Morse looked in to say that the Lieutenant would like to speak to Mr. Gamadge.

Windorp stood beside a large round table near the front windows of the library, four books arranged before him in the light of a shaded lamp. He said without preamble: "We found these and the script of some novel, it looked like, in a drawer in the office, locked up."

"Yes; I locked 'em. They're part of that story I was going to tell you; the job I was called in on."

"Miss Burt had some mixed-up tale or other."

"I'll explain as well as I can." Gamadge produced Chapter Nine, and handed it to him. Then he sat down, Windorp sat down, and between them they studied the case of Poe, Herbert, Ford, and Christopher Marlowe vs. Florence Hutter Mason.

"It's a queer set-up," said Windorp at last, "queer from the word go. Is Mrs. Deedes in her right mind?"

"Yes; but seeking distraction in byways of the spirit."

"You mean spirits. All this about that planchette board and Mr. Hutter's wooden idols. And I understand she has her divorced husband living with her secretly."

"Yes. Miss Burt just now informed us that she had been saving trouble for you."

Windorp looked sharply at him. "Think she's telling the truth?"

"So far as she knows it, and so far as it concerns others."

"She says Miss Wing, the secretary, put these things into Mrs. Mason's novel out of spite."

"That is probably not true. They weren't put in out of spite by Miss Wing; they may have been put in to raise Miss Wing's legacy from thousands to millions."

Windorp sat back to stare.

"That's why, Hutter being dead and the millions at Mrs. Mason's disposal, I persuaded her to make yet another will. Robert Macloud, her lawyer, is coming up to-night; I thought he might as well inform the beneficiaries that Mrs. Mason's death wouldn't make a millionaire of anybody."

"Burbage told me your ideas about the nurses and the specially prepared food. I get it. But this—" he fingered the pages of Chapter Nine—"this will business means that the Wing girl is guilty."

"No; a friend may have been working for her, or Mason may have thought himself still the residuary legatee."

"Miss Wing says she was down in that walled garden from

NOTHING CAN RESCUE ME   125

a quarter to three until five past, when she saw Percy. But it's no alibi for either of them; the whole murder could have been over and done with in five minutes, and the doctor thinks it happened, or probably happened, at the early end of that forty minutes—between the time you left Hutter and the time you found him."

"I'm beginning to feel more and more certain that it was over as early as three o'clock."

"As for Wing and Percy—why should the murderer go down to that place at all?"

"That's what I'm asking myself. Look here; Miss Wing wouldn't have said she saw Percy if she didn't think she saw him; he had only to contradict her, as he has contradicted her. She saw somebody, though. I wish you'd have Percy in and ask him to show us his hat and coat."

Windorp, after a frowning look at Gamadge, went to the door; he spoke to Sergeant Morse, who was stationed just outside it, and came back again. A minute later Percy entered the library.

"Mr. Percy," said Gamadge, "Lieutenant Windorp and I would be very much obliged if you'd introduce us to your coat and hat."

Percy, his hands in his trouser pockets, looked from him to Windorp. "Delighted," he said. "Follow me."

They went, a procession of three, out of the library and down the hall. Percy opened a door next the office, and led the way into a large cloakroom, from which opened a flower room and a commodious lavatory

Percy went to the row of hangers, above which a long shelf held an assortment of hats. He pushed tweeds and finer cloths aside, glanced at the shelf, rummaged thereon, and at last turned a blank face to the others. "They're not here."

"In your room, perhaps?" Windorp was not taking the matter too seriously.

"They're not in my room. And if they'd been taken away and brushed, they'd have been put back again."

"Call Thomas," suggested Windorp.

"No need to call him," said Gamadge. "I thought they'd be missing, and I think I know where they are."

"Well, then, where are they?" Percy looked completely puzzled. "I'm rather interested, you know, because the dear old coat is the only winter coat I have."

"I suppose they're in the walled garden, Miss Wing saw somebody in them, over a hedge, perhaps, and thought it was you."

"Saw somebody?"

"The murderer, you know."

Windorp, suddenly galvanized into passionate interest, said: "But that means Mason, if it doesn't mean Mr. Percy here."

"A lady can wear a man's coat and hat."

"Wore a man's coat over her skirt? That would be a fine disguise, I must say!"

"A lady can wear slacks. I dare say she could roll up her skirt and wear it too; in fact, that's what she must have done if my theory's correct. I don't insist on a woman, you know; it may," he said, glancing at Percy, "have been a man."

"Kindly tell me," begged Percy, "why the murderer should have taken a walk in the garden in slacks and my coat and hat."

"Well—to dispose of the slacks."

Windorp's complexion of old brick slowly reddened to the colour of new brick. He said after a moment: "I suppose you mean they may have been worn to commit the murder in, and got bloodstained."

"Yes, and they'd make too bulky a bundle to be carried around the place under an arm, or disposed of indoors. What I think is that the shorter raincoat—Hutter's, I believe—was worn because the other, Mason's, is one of those heavy rustling affairs that would make considerable noise in a quiet room. The bloodstains on it are low; one of the griffons seems to have got blood on its paw, which may mean that the stains were even lower than the hem of the raincoat—those little dogs don't jump high. When the murderer opened the cupboard door a second time—"

"I get it, I get it."

"My idea is that the murderer disposed of the slacks in the walled garden, left Percy's coat and hat there, and returned to the house undisguised. Why not? Miss Wing did so, Miss Hutter did so, Mason did so—"

Windorp swung to the door of the cloakroom, and pushed through.

"And nobody saw any of them come home." Gamadge seized his own hat and coat and followed him into the back hall. "The murder didn't take *five* minutes, Windorp; it must have taken all of thirty-five, counting the trip to the walled garden and the disposal of the slacks."

Percy also snatched a topcoat from a rack. "I only hope my things weren't disposed of too," he said anxiously, hurrying after the others through the swing door.

CHAPTER TWELVE

A Garden Not So Lovesome

SCANDINAVIAN ACCENTS ISSUED from the servants' sitting-room of the passage on the left, but no servant was in sight. The procession—Windorp, Gamadge, and Percy, the latter struggling into a coat too small for him—passed the kitchen door and the pantry service window, and through the back door of the house into wet darkness. "Beaver?" called Windorp.

A torch flashed in their faces. Beaver's huge bulk, towering behind it, stood solid for a moment and then moved aside.

"Take us down to that walled garden," said Windorp. The torch lighted slippery bricks, and guided the party down an inclined walk which ran straight for twenty yards and then forked to the left. This bypath led them between great yew hedges, dripping wet. Except for the steady gleam of Beaver's light it was in utter darkness, the dark of a narrow tunnel whose roof is a clouded night sky.

"The path down to this alley isn't overlooked from the kitchen," said Gamadge, "because the kitchen yard is hedged in too. It's overlooked by the dining-room, but who looks out of dining-room windows at three in the afternoon? Mrs. Mason's back windows are heavily curtained, and she doesn't sit beside either of them; she uses the ones on the north and south sides of her room. Miss Hutter and Mr. Percy were not looking out of their windows between three and three-thirty, I presume."

"I wasn't," said Percy.

"Miss Hutter says she came back from her walk at three-fifteen, or about that," growled Windorp. "Didn't see anybody at all. Came in the back way and went up the back stairs to her room and took a nap."

They were steadily descending, and bearing to the south; the watery murmur of the stream increased to a subdued roar.

"The walled garden must practically overhang the old swimming-pool," said Gamadge.

"It does," Percy told him. "How I implored Mrs. Mason to have the place open on the water-side; but no, she had seen something in Istanbul."

"The Hutters see such unfortunate things," said Gamadge. "Old Benjamin saw a country house on Long Island, didn't he?"

"Within driving distance of the city. Yes, he did. Sylvanus used to laugh about the geraniums and the grape-vine trellis," replied Percy, "but I thought that a walled garden was far less suitable to the scene. However."

"They incinerate down here some place," rumbled Beaver.

Windorp stopped dead. "What's that you say?"

"They burn rubbish. I smelt it when we got there this afternoon, but it's damped out now."

Windorp, with a kind of howl, bumped into him. But with only one torch, and that in the hand of the guide, there was small hope of mending the pace. Beaver introduced them cautiously into an ambiguous region of arched walls and hedges, wide grey spaces, and looming spires of evergreen.

"Here we are in the middle," said Percy, as they passed beneath still another dripping arch, "and there's the pool."

They stood looking down into a deep, oblong excavation surrounded by shallow steps. From the middle of the concrete rose a bronze group which seemed, by the light of Beaver's torch, to represent somebody fighting a large fish.

"Lovely in summer," Percy informed them. "Goldfish, pond lilies, everything. The flower-beds around the brim—"

"I want the incinerator," said Windorp.

"It was over there, I thought." Beaver gestured towards the south-west corner of the garden, and Percy remarked that something could have been burned in one of the urns.

"There are four," he said, "one at each corner, just inside the wall. The outer hedge and the wall form a nice broad walk. Shady in summer; this whole place is overhung with trees."

"I remember the trees down here," said Gamadge, "and I hate to think that any of them were rooted up."

"Oh, they were," said Percy.

He preceded Beaver across the wide central space, through the inner hedge, and through the outer one; then, turning right, he led the party to a tall and broad-based urn, set into the angle of the wall. Stumbling, he complained: "Here's the tarpaulin. The urns are covered by tarpaulins all winter."

Windorp peered over the fluted brim of the great vase, while Beaver directed the beam of his torch upon a dense and bitter-smelling heap of black ashes.

"I guess you win, Mr. Gamadge," said Windorp. "Beaver, you cover this up. Perhaps there's something left of the thing, whatever it was."

Beaver said: "The stone in there looks greasy to me. I think benzine was used perhaps."

"A lot can be done with ashes."

Percy had been hunting along the hedges; he now emitted a loud, wailing cry, and exclaimed: "My coat and hat! Stuffed under the hedge here, and the hat's sopping! Sopping!"

"I'll take those." Windorp snatched the garments out of his arms.

"Enough to ruin them," said Percy, "and what's more, enough to ruin the hedge. Of all the vandals!"

Gamadge said: "If there's a garden tap about—"

"There is; right here."

"Then perhaps water was carried to the smouldering ashes in your hat."

"Well," said Percy, "one thing at least is fairly obvious; I wasn't the party who wore the coat and hat down here this afternoon, and was seen by Miss Wing. I can't afford to stuff my clothes under hedges and carry water in my only hat."

Windorp looked at him; in the light of Beaver's torch both faces flickered oddly—pale, distorted masks. "The thing that's obvious to me," he said, "is this: only one person knew that this garden wasn't a place to be seen in this afternoon; and that person would deny being seen here. Miss Wing might think it was an alibi; one person knew it was exactly the opposite."

Beaver's moving torch gave Percy a crooked smile. "I can go you one better," he said. "If wore my own coat and hat down here, why didn't I wear them back to the house again? They constituted no disguise for me."

Gamadge did not wait to hear what Windorp would make of this; he found his way as well as he could through the hedges, across the open space, through hedges and wall on the farther side, and up the yew walk. He entered the house, reached the back stairs via the swing door, and mounted to the second story. On that landing he paused; sounds of woe came to him from Louise's room above.

He climbed to the third floor, and looked in at her open doorway. She had comfortable quarters, nicely furnished, and equipped with a radio, a phonograph, an electric heater, and a sewing machine. Louise sat in her armchair, crying.

"Don't feel like that!" he begged her.

She raised a crumpled yellow face to him. "*Still* zey won't let me see Madame!"

"Who won't?"

"Les infirmières. Les infirmières."

"You how what nurses are."

"If Madame is to travel to-morrow, I must get her zings ready. I must look over her underzings and her stuggings."

"Why not?"

"We are shut out—Dodo and Bobo and I."

Gamadge now saw that the griffons were curled up together beside the radiator. He said: "Great friends, the three of you. Belgian, aren't they? I suppose you converse with them in French."

"And take zem for walks."

"You come along with me, the lot of you!"

They made a bustling progress downstairs to Mrs. Mason's door. Miss Mudge opened it to Gamadge's rap, disclosing a scene of cosiness amounting to gaiety. Firelight danced, lamps shed a rosy glow; a second and stouter nurse was busy over an electric plate in a corner. Mrs. Deedes, on a chair between the twin beds, supervised the activities of Mrs. Mason; and Mrs. Mason, prettily dressed in a pink bed-jacket and wearing a lace cap with lace strings, was working hard at planchette; the board which supported it was propped across her knees.

Mrs. Deedes, looking up, met Gamadge's incredulous gaze with a disarming smile. She said; "It amuses her."

"Oh? I hope she's doing it reverently. Sally, I think you're mad."

"Oh, Henry," exclaimed Mrs. Mason, her eyes sparkling and her cheeks flushed, "I almost got a word!"

"Where did you get planchette?"

"That nice Ridley found it somewhere for us." Gamadge, remembering where planchette had last been used at Underhill, frowned heavily. Mrs. Deedes said: "Don't be cross," and Miss Mudge said that it couldn't possibly hurt Mrs. Mason to play Ouija, it was lots of fun.

"Planchette isn't Ouija," said Gamadge. "Planchette has been writing for nearly a hundred years—before Ouija was ever heard of. Louise wants to come in and do some packing or something, Florence."

"Why, Louise, where have you been? You haven't been near me." Mrs. Mason did not take her eyes from planchette, and Louise, scuttling past Gamadge, immediately buried herself in the depths of a large dress-closet. The griffons pranced across the room and scrambled up on the bed; Mrs. Mason welcomed them rapturously and planchette slid to the floor.

"Louise is a privileged party," Gamadge explained to Miss Mudge. She nodded, and said in a low voice: "Mrs. Mason *will* see people. At first she wouldn't, but now she lets everybody come."

"Keep an eye on them; don't let anything worry her."

"No, we won't."

Gamadge went to his room, and found that somebody had found time to lay out his evening clothes; life, it seemed, was to go on as usual at Underhill. Reflecting that Sylvanus would have approved, Gamadge enjoyed a hot bath and a leisurely toilet; then he wandered through into Sylvanus's large corner room. He switched on a light.

Sylvanus, like many other collectors, had cared little for schemes of decoration. His best things were no doubt crated and waiting for burial; the few treasures he had kept about him here were not arranged according to any period or plan. Paintings— in their original gilt frames—hung crowded on the walls; the floor was covered—more than covered, for one end of it had had to be rolled under the window seat—by an old and ugly Persian rug. Buhl, oak, and marquetry furniture—each piece no doubt a bargain—showed that Sylvanus's tastes ran to the remarkable rather than to the beautiful. On the mantelpiece two black and ancient wooden figures, primitive and horrifying, stood among jade tear-bottles and ornaments of Sèvres and Saxe.

Gamadge went up and studied the African images. They were symbols, no doubt; but of what? Those misshapen limbs and features that melted so indistinguishably into one another had been vividly rendered; one could hardly believe that they had not been seen with waking eyes, or imagine what experience could have transmuted them into a dream. He wondered whether the sculptor had known what the effect of them would be, and whether he could have understood evil, as modern people understand it, at all.

At a sound from the doorway he turned. Evelyn Wing stood there, very handsome in a dark-green dinner dress with a high neck and long sleeves; it made her look older than she had looked in day clothes, or perhaps it was Hutter's death that had given her that gravity, that mature, careworn expression.

She asked: "Ought they to leave this room unlocked? I thought they locked rooms up, when people died—like that."

"They lock up the rooms they die in."

"Mr. Hutter worked at this desk." She put her hand on a big carved-oak secretaire.

"Weren't his important papers downstairs in the office files?"

"I don't know what he had here. I could see."

"You may be sure that the police have seen."

"Would they mind my looking? I did his accounts for him."

"Windorp might be glad of your help."

She still hesitated, and he waited in silence. At last she said: "There seem to be so many strangers in the house. I shouldn't like the servants to be blamed if anything disappeared."

"I fancy Hutter's valuables are safe enough."

"Nobody but dealers will care about them now. Poor, kind little man."

"You're the first person I've heard speak of him like that."

"They're probably too much distressed to speak of him. I'm an outsider. He was always nice to me."

"The extraordinary part of it, though," said Gamadge, leaning up against the footboard of the canopied bed, "is that the manner of his going seems to distress them so little. It doesn't impress you, so far as I can see. Yet there's a murderer—a ferocious and brutal murderer in the house, whose motive for murder is obscure."

She frowned at him. "I suppose we can't take it in; if it's true."

"It's true enough."

"I supposed that somebody had had a terrible quarrel with him. That *can* happen, but it doesn't seem exactly like murder to me."

"It's usually manslaughter; but this wasn't. Hutter was struck down from behind, with every circumstance of premeditation."

She put out a hand and steadied herself against the door frame. "I meant the quarrel must have been earlier."

"Still, I should think you'd all feel very uncomfortable with such a violent party loose on the premises. I'm not comfortable about this murder, I can assure you. I have a very nasty feeling about it. Cold-blooded sort of thing, and sly—very sly. Elements of desperation about it, too; the party cut it very fine. Unpleasant to know that it must be connected with that business about Mrs. Mason's novel."

She raised her eyes slowly to his. "It simply can't be."

"It simply must be. And that hocus-pocus with her novel—do you know how it affected me from the time I first heard of it?" He jerked his head towards the mantelpiece. "Like those African images there. Pure evil. A murder, a brutal murder, is no more than the natural outcome of evil like that, and not half so frightening."

She said faintly: "You exaggerate. You don't understand what extraordinary things some people do when they're angry. They're like children, smashing things. Those sculptures— they're like that; just done for their own sake."

"They weren't done for their own—or art's sake; and neither was that business with Mrs. Mason's book. Murder followed it. Really, Miss Wing, I don't understand you people at all. I congratulate you all on your nerve. I'm going down the hall to say good-night to Mrs. Mason, and I assure you I hate the idea of all the closed doors I shall pass on my way—two of them belonging to cupboards, you know."

She forced a smile. "I don't know why you should be in any danger; or why I should."

"No, and that's a very interesting thing too, because it looked, on the face of it, as if you were meant to be injured by that trick with Mrs. Mason's book."

"But you said it really wasn't done to injure me."

"I theorized. Can you be so sure why it wasn't done?"

She turned away, and he followed her into the hall. Mrs. Deedes, coming out of her room across the landing, faced them droopingly. She wore a long, filmy grey dress with frill sleeves, and the antique pearls were in her ears and around her neck. She said: "I do want a cocktail. Will you see that we get a cocktail, Henry?"

"I will, if I have to mix them myself."

Susie Burt came along from her room. Her flaming hair was thickly curled on her shoulders, and she wore a long white dress with a round neck. She said: "Oh, I'm glad you all dressed. I didn't know what to do."

"One changes for dinner, I suppose. This thing is for any hour of the day." Mrs. Deedes spoke vaguely, and began to descend the stairs.

"It's lovely." Susie Burt followed. Miss Wing stood aside for her, and then went down in her turn. Gamadge started for Mrs. Mason's room; half-way along the hall Mason came hurrying towards him, his fingers at his tie. He said sharply "Gamadge, I wish you'd be good enough to tell me what all this is about. They're boiling eggs in Florence's room, and heating soup out of cans. They've had special milk in. Has Burbage gone crazy?"

"Don't you really see any sense in it?" asked Gamadge mildly.

"Not unless Burbage thinks she's in for a serious illness, and needs a diet of slops."

"She'll be all right when she's away from here."

"She's not going away."

"Why should you object to her going?"

"We'll both clear out in a few days. She'll not go without me. I won't have it."

"You can't go yet, Mason, as you know very well. Do you want your wife in the same house with a maniac?"

Mason opened his mouth, closed it, and plunged off down the hall. Percy came around the corner from the back stairs; beautiful in his dinner clothes, his black hair shining.

"My next-door neighbour Miss Hutter," he told Gamadge, "is nibbling food from a tray on her bureau. Isn't she allowed at table? I feel as though I were sharing the attic with the family idiot."

"Not having been invited to the house-party," said Gamadge, "Miss Hutter probably wishes to efface herself."

"At least she can't decently share my bath. If there's one thing I abominate," said Percy, "it's the sight of other people's tooth paste."

"I hope the police got her some tooth paste."

"It's ridiculous to coop poor old Corinne up with the rest of us murderers."

"You'll be glad you're cooped up when to-morrow comes. Underhill will be in a state of siege."

Percy gave the characteristic hunch of his shoulders that was not quite a shrug, and went on down the hall to the front stairs. Gamadge knocked at Mrs. Mason's door; the smiling Miss Mudge opened it, and invited him in.

CHAPTER THIRTEEN

Lighting

ALL LIGHTS WERE ON, AND MISS MOYLAN, the stout nurse, was preparing Mrs. Mason's supper with the help of the electric plate. Mrs. Mason, a tray across her knees, looked happy and childlike in the pink jacket and the lace cap, of which the strings were now tied under her chin. She waved her fruit spoon at Gamadge.

"I'm ever so much better, Henry," she cried, "but Dr. Burbage wants me to be careful for a day or two, so Miss Moylan's cooking for me."

"Pretty nice, by the smell of it." Gamadge went up to the bed, and leaned on the footboard to look at her.

"And Louise has found me something black to wear, isn't it lucky?"

Louise, her arms heaped with delicate black raiment, ducked her head at him, smiling.

"And we were out of sugar and things; Johnny Ridley had

to go to Erasmus for them. Imagine!" Mrs. Mason swallowed a spoonful of grapefruit. Gamadge thought: Sylvanus wouldn't have behaved like this if Florence had died; no, he wouldn't. But Florence had had an additional quarter of a century in which to be so petted and pampered that she no longer cared what people thought of her; even so, she was not perhaps entirely frivolous—there was perhaps no middle course for her between delirious high spirits and utter collapse.

He said: "I'm glad you're so cheerful here."

"If people would only understand that it does no good to any one to be depressed! Corinne stopped in to see me, but she's the type that loves to talk about death and funerals, and I couldn't bear it. That reminds me, Louise; you'll have to find something of Miss Wing's for her to wear to-night. They're making her stay."

"Mees Wing has gone downstairs. Must I—"

"No, just get something out of the dresser and closet and bathroom." Louise trotted away, and Florence went on: "Dr. Burbage says I simply mustn't be worried. He's making all the arrangements."

"That's good."

"Tim was so difficult about my going to town to-morrow. He's so selfish." Mrs. Mason consumed grapefruit, and continued plaintively: "Somebody must stay here to look after the place, especially if rowdies and lunatics are going to break in. I'm *sure* it was a rowdy or a lunatic, Henry."

"Windorp will round the rowdies and lunatics up."

"Evelyn came and sat with me a long time. She always knows just what to say and do; she's such a comfort to me."

Gamadge's eye fell upon planchette, retrieved from the floor, and now perched—he thought with a rather watchful and alert look about it—on top of the desk. He said: "And isn't Sally?"

"Yes, but I always think young people are so much more stimulating; when one's in trouble, you know. Glen Percy came in to cheer me up. He's always so sweet and so funny." The nurses began to giggle, and Mrs. Mason, giggling herself, went on: "Those pets of his he's always talking about—I know he makes them up! He told us about two lovebirds he had once that hated each other, and he couldn't understand it, and finally they both laid an egg!"

Gamadge joined in the hearty laughter that followed. "And then Susie came," said Mrs. Mason, "all dressed up for dinner. Rather bad taste, I thought, and I think it's absurd for a girl of her age to wear her hair down her back."

"Perhaps you told her so?"

"Yes, I did; she has no mother to tell her things. I only wish she had; I only wish Caroline were alive to keep her in order."

Gamadge dimly remembered ferocious combats between Florence Mason and her friend the late Mrs. Burt. He echoed Florence's sigh.

"Now, eat your grapefruit," said Miss Moylan. "Then you'll have consommé, and I'm making you a lovely sauce for your egg."

"You'll do, Florrie," smiled Gamadge. "Good night, and I'll see you in the morning."

"You see how they're spoiling me," she said gleefully; and added—perhaps to herself, perhaps to the nurses—as he left the room: "Oh dear, I forgot again. Well, I'll just do it now, that's all!"

Miss Mudge closed the door. As Gamadge moved away from it, Officer Ridley came down the back stairs.

"On patrol, are you?" asked Gamadge. "That's good."

"Yes, sir. I'm spelling Beaver while he eats his supper."

Gamadge entered the drawing-room to find that cocktails had been served, and that the well-dressed group about the fireplace seemed to be consuming them in absolute silence. Percy alone sat apart; he was striking low chords on the piano, his cocktail balanced in front of the music rack. Gamadge went to the console on which the shaker had been left, and poured himself a brimming glassful of Martini.

Percy looked up to remark in an undertone: "What a fellow you are. You have dreams, and the dreams come true. Those ashes are on their way to Windorp's laboratory in Bethea."

"Did you get your coat and hat back?" asked Gamadge.

"Hat, yes; coat, no. The ridiculous creatures are looking for bloodstains on it; they think it may have rubbed on the slacks. They say it's longer than Hutter's mackintosh. I don't know why you're so set on the idea of slacks."

"Do you prefer the idea of an extra skirt, worn outside the usual one? Slacks have no gender; I'm leaving the question open to include the men."

"Gallant of you," said Percy, and was going to add something, when he, as well as Gamadge and the whole party turned a shocked face towards the hall. For ten seconds it was a roomful of waxwork; then Gamadge was out of the door and up the stairs, and the frightful cry had ceased. What a cry it had been, he thought, to reach them through Florence Mason's door; he had no doubt, not for an instant, that it was her voice which had uttered it.

As Windorp and Sergeant Morse burst from the library a succession of louder, more human shrieks came to them from the upper hall: "Doctor. Telephone. Somebody." Miss Mudge stood outside Mrs. Mason's door and repeated the words wildly, in crescendo. Gamadge, hurtling past her, almost ran into Corinne Hutter; she was in the room at his heels.

At first all Gamadge could see were the broad backs of Ridley and Miss Moylan, leaning over the bed. Miss Mudge, pushing her way in with Windorp, who had her by the arm, was now crying; "She can't be gone. Not in two seconds, she can't be gone."

"Gone? Gone?" Windorp dropped her arm and made for the bedside. He shouted over his shoulder; "Get that door shut," and Morse herded the crowd back and closed the door in their faces. "Gone?" repeated Windorp, staring down at the bed.

"She was just starting her soup, a new can of soup," sobbed Miss Mudge. "She just screamed—screamed and died."

"For God's sake"—Windorp addressed the stout nurse, who seemed to be in a state of iron calm—"what happened to her?"

"Nothing," sobbed Miss Mudge, and Miss Moylan turned on her in violent contempt. "Nothing but cyanide," she said. "You fool, couldn't you *smell*?"

Ridley shifted a little, and Gamadge had a glimpse of the destruction on the bed before Miss Moylan pulled the eiderdown over it. "She must have taken something," barked Windorp.

"Only what we gave her," replied Miss Moylan. "I couldn't believe my senses. She didn't have one thing."

"Except those capsules," sobbed Miss Mudge.

"Capsules?" Windorp rounded on her "What capsules?"

"That's so." The stout nurse looked suddenly shaken. "But they were just iron pills, Mudge told me."

"Her iron pills; Dr. Burbage gave them to her last year when she had flu, and she's taken them ever since. Four a day," Miss Mudge gabbled. "Two after breakfast and two after dinner, and she always forgot the dinner ones, and she took them when she remembered, and she—"

"That's right." Miss Moylan's expression of astonishment and doubt was almost ludicrous. "She took two just when this gentleman here left the room."

Gamadge nodded. Miss Mudge went babbling on: "It's Dr. Burbage's own prescription, you can read it on the bottle. She kept them in her night-table drawer."

The bottle was produced from the night-table drawer; it contained a few large red capsules, and Windorp, holding it by the tips of his fingers, said: "There are four in this."

"Yes, she said she'd have to get it filled; I mean, get another bottle." Miss Moylan had regained her stony calm.

"A couple of nurses in the room," said Windorp, "and a trooper outside the door, and this happens."

Corinne Hutter, her face chalk-white, had stood beside Gamadge without moving. Now she spoke, looking at him:

"I didn't know anything could kill anybody like that."

Gamadge said: "I think cyanide can, on top of acid. She had been eating grapefruit. I suppose I'm a fool, but I feel as if I'd fed her the stuff with my own hands."

Windorp said: "We don't know yet if the stuff was…" he removed the screw-top of the bottle, and sniffed. "Can't smell anything. Morse, you get on the telephone. Get Burbage too. Miss Hutter, there's going to be all kinds of an upset in the house from now on, unless somebody takes hold. You say you ran the place once, when you were housekeeper or something. Can you do it again?"

"I guess so."

"Quiet the servants down, all that. You do the best you can, will you?"

She nodded, cast another strained look at the heap beneath the blue and pink satin coverlet, and walked from the room. Morse had already vanished. Gamadge, watching Lieutenant Windorp wrap the bottle of capsules in a piece of cellophane which Miss Moylan found for him, wasted no thoughts on the irony of the situation. His defences had not crumbled—they had enclosed the victim in an area already mined. He was concerned now only with what was left for him to do; what he must do before he quitted Underhill.

Morse put his head into the room. "You nurses got any brandy? Mr. Mason's collapsed here in the hall."

"Get my flask out of my bag, Mudge," directed Miss Moylan. "*It* won't poison him."

"And there's a gentleman just come, asking for Mr. Gamadge," said Morse. "Name's Macloud. Expects to spend the night."

The next hour or two was afterwards vague to Gamadge; but he at length found himself, his head cleared by coffee, sitting at the round table in the library with Windorp, Macloud, and Dr Burbage. The coffee and sandwiches on the table constituted the only dinner that any of them had had. The bottle containing four red capsules stood in front of Burbage, open; he held one of the capsules in his hand, and a pair of tweezers in the other

"Hydrocyanic acid crystals," he said, "in every one of these. Not enough to change the colour of the preparation, but enough to kill anybody."

Macloud, who had been sitting well down on his spine, pipe in mouth, eyes fixed on Gamadge with some commiseration, now said: "I didn't know even hydrocyanic acid killed like lightning."

"It does when hydrocyanic gas is set free," Burbage informed him gloomily, "and gas was set free in this case. Mrs. Mason had citric acid in her stomach. When the capsules melted, the cyanide crystals poured into the acid, gas was set free, and she died a death that isn't much slower than lightning."

"And if she hadn't happened to be eating grapefruit she might have been saved?"

"Doubt it; slim chance. As it was, all the doctors and nurses and hospitals there are couldn't have saved her; but she didn't just happen to be eating grapefruit, Mr. Macloud."

"No?"

Burbage shook his head. "That's one of the ghastly things about the case. She always did have grapefruit before her dinner. She'd been told it was good for her, she liked it, and the result was that she never missed it."

Windorp said: "Somebody knew she wouldn't have a chance. Somebody knew her habits, and read up all the dope on the poison. She didn't take two of the capsules you gave her after breakfast, Doctor; she forgot the breakfast ones, and took them after lunch. I have two witnesses for that—her maid, Louise

Baugnon, and the girl that brought coffee to her in her room. Those two capsules were all right. When were the poisoned ones substituted? Because of course poisoned ones had been prepared beforehand—there wouldn't have been time to refill."

Macloud again spoke; "I suppose you can get these capsules without a prescription?"

"Get 'em in these bottles of eighty-four at any drugstore," said Burbage. "They're put out in this quantity by the wholesalers."

"And how does one procure hydrocyanic acid for purposes of murder?"

Windorp said: "Sylvanus Hutter was a photographer, and they tell me a mighty good one; his own pictures are in his books. I shouldn't have thought he'd develop, but Thomas says he still did, now and then, when he snapped a view or something around here. He has a dark room in the basement—"

"Remember it well," said Macloud. "Shouldn't have asked the question."

"Yes, but there was everything for developing in the cupboard there except cyanide," continued Windorp. "Thomas said he thought there had been a little bottle with a pinch or two of the crystals in it, but it's gone. The cupboard was locked, by the way; one of those locks you can open with a penknife. Morse did."

Gamadge broke his long silence. "The capsules were changed," he said, "between four-fifteen and four-thirty this afternoon, approximate figures; when we had Mrs. Mason downstairs, Windorp, to break the news of Hutter's death to her."

Windorp raised sombre eyes to his. "She was alone in her room after lunch, between the time your conference broke up and about three, when you saw her. She might have had her back turned, or she might have stepped into the bathroom."

"I don't think anybody would have risked that, Windorp."

"Every last one of these people was with her afterwards;

most of 'em sat in that little chair between the twin beds, with the night-table right beside."

"And both nurses hovering, as Mrs. Deedes said, like bats; and Florence Mason beside the night-table too. She was very sharp, Windorp; careless and forgetful, but very sharp, and she detested liberties of any kind. I shouldn't back a conjuror to have opened that drawer, and taken out that bottle, and changed the capsules that were in it for poisoned ones. No, it was done during that fifteen minutes when the room was empty; and when all the people concerned were anywhere, so far as we know."

Windorp looked baffled. "And how am I to save them from one another without locking 'em all up? And how am I to do that? I'll have a steady patrol night and day, and I'll work out something with the county; and I shan't leave the place myself, not with a mass-murderer loose, and no evidence against a soul."

"Not even a bloodstain on Percy's coat?" asked Gamadge.

"Not a bloodstain on anybody, or anything, except the things we were meant to see. And no cyanide in the house, so far as we can tell without sawing it into slices. I'm not going to do that; it's not hard to dispose of a pinch of cyanide crystals—or hide 'em, either."

Macloud took his pipe out of his mouth. "I shall have great pleasure," he said, "in reading Florence's last will and testament to our friends in the drawing-room."

"They're in there waiting for you." Windorp added: "And a worse collection of poker faces you never saw."

"Let us see what impression the will makes on them. There may be rejoicing, but not such as will be known in the Church of SS. Gervase and Protase in New York, and the Bethea Home for Destitute Children. My friend Gamadge thinks that he has made a failure of this case; but I beg to differ with him. Sylvanus and Florence Mason would certainly have been murdered if he hadn't been here, and Miss Evelyn Wing, a young person in no way related to the Hutters, would now be in possession of about ten million dollars and Underhill. Really, Gamadge, I think you ought to be congratulated."

Windorp said: "Nobody's blaming him. All these people except Percy come in for big legacies, though; bigger than they were before. Mason—he's heading for a breakdown, if you ask me. I don't know—I suppose he did marry Mrs. Mason for her money, and I suppose he's no angel, but I wouldn't have thought he'd use poison. If he did it his motive must have been stronger than money even."

"You put it delicately, Windorp." Macloud smiled, and rose. "I guess it's hard to know what a man will do when he's bowled right over."

"It's impossible to know; as a lawyer, I can assure you of that."

"I'll sit in on this will-reading." Windorp also got to his feet. "I'll be in the dining-room."

Burbage picked up his bag. "Mind if I give those two unfortunate women a lift home? The nurses."

"Not at all, if you'll see that they get to the inquest."

"I only hope this won't hurt professionally," grumbled the doctor.

"Don't know why it should."

"If it ever comes to a trial, some defence lawyer will have it that Florence Mason was killed by a mistake on the part of her doctor, her druggist, or her trained nurses. You'll see."

CHAPTER FOURTEEN

Last Will

THE PARTY IN THE DRAWING-ROOM had resolved itself into its elements. Mason sat tipped back against the wall on the right of the dining-room door, arms folded and chin on chest. His colour was bad; he looked like a man half-stunned. Percy stood facing the hearth. His hands gripped the mantel ledge, and his eyes were on the embers of the neglected fire. Susie Burt had curled down into a corner of the big sofa until only the crown of her head was visible above its rounded back. Evelyn Wing stood beside a table between the east windows; she turned the pages of a magazine slowly, as if counting them. Mrs. Deedes—Gamadge stopped in the doorway to stare at her—was again occupied with planchette. Rescued from yet another chamber of death, it had been placed on the console that had held the cocktail tray; she stood looking down on it, one long hand poised above it like a hand of wax.

Corinne Hutter, upright on the piano bench, brooded over

them all—a homely but implacable Fate. In her grey cardigan jacket and brown skirt, her brown stockings and neat Oxfords, she might have been the denizen of another world, come to judge these wasters and parasites. But there was no anger in her face; she studied them dispassionately, with the intelligent gaze whose steadiness Gamadge had come to recognize as formidable.

Mason looking up as the newcomers entered the room, seemed for the first time to notice what Mrs. Deedes was doing, and addressed her harshly: "Stop that ghastly nonsense, Sally, or I'll put the thing in the fire."

"Does it annoy you? I'm sorry, Tim." She moved away from the console.

"Annoy me? It bores me. There's nobody to read those messages of yours now," he said, looking at her with a smile. "Nobody to act on their suggestions any more."

"I don't know what you mean." She walked slowly to the sofa, and sat down in the corner opposite Susie Burt. Percy turned, left the hearth as Macloud approached it, and found himself a chair. Gamadge joined Corinne Hutter on the piano bench. She glanced at him, raised her eyebrows in a faint but expressive look of doubt or bafflement, and then concentrated her interest on Macloud.

That gentleman had a long, narrow face, a long nose, eyes set well back under thick brows, and a square chin; he was the scourge of venal or shifty witnesses, and an abomination to tricky lawyers. He said: "Sorry to keep you people out of your beds, but I thought you might as well hear Florence's will."

Mason said carelessly, like a man no longer concerned with civilities: "I thought Syl and Florence got rid of you."

Macloud looked at him calmly. "Florence re-engaged me to-day, after Sylvanus was murdered." He took the will from an inside breast-pocket.

Corinne Hutter asked: "Do you want me here, Mr. Macloud? I'm not down in Cousin Florence's will."

"Excuse me, Corinne, you are."

"I am?"

"You're down for a nice little annuity—a thousand dollars a year."

Gamadge had seldom seen anyone more surprised: "There's some mistake."

"None, I assure you."

"I can't take it. I promised my father—"

"Accept the advice of a seasoned man of law, Corinne, and forget all that old history. It belongs to another world," said Macloud. "You'll be glad of this money. Anything can happen in these days, and the library in Erasmus may very well change into something else over night." He opened the will, but he was again interrupted. Percy addressed him in his soft, unemphatic voice:

"At least I'm not down for anything, sir; am I to sit in on this? I'd rather not, if it's all the same to you."

"You stay right here, Glen Percy." Gamadge wondered, hearing those tuneless accents, how the owner of Corinne Hutter's voice and the owner of Percy's could possibly belong to the same race.

"I beg your pardon?" Percy turned to look at her as at a minor portent.

"Oblige the lady." Macloud's saturnine mouth curved upwards at a corner.

"Glad to," said Percy, "and glad, if I may say so, to hear Miss Hutter's voice raised at last in authority. I take off my hat to her— or would if I were wearing one. I don't think anybody else could have kept this establishment in order to-day, upstairs and down."

"Thanks," said Corinne drily.

A shadow, imperceptible except to a watcher, had moved across the shadowy depths of the dining-room. Macloud saw it, and addressed Mason: "I'm extremely sorry to disturb you, but this room is a big one, you're rather far away, and one doesn't care to shout. Would you draw up a bit?"

Mason, with a lurch and a stumble, got himself out of his chair and across the room. He sank down on the sofa between Mrs. Deedes and Miss Burt, ignoring both of them. Suddenly, as Macloud flattened the scrawled pages of Mrs. Mason's last will, he asked in a loud voice:

"What's that?"

"What's what?" Macloud looked down at him.

"That thing in your hand. That's not Florence's will. Her will is typed—you drew it up yourself."

"That's ancient history, Mason," said Macloud, viewing him steadily. "The will you refer to was made three years ago; there have been two since then, neither of them drawn up by me. This one was signed and duly witnessed this afternoon, within an hour of Hutter's death."

"She made a new will to-day?" Mason's voice caught in his throat.

"Naturally. Her nephew's death changed her financial status. She had a large fortune to dispose of from the moment he died."

Mason seemed dazed. He turned to look over his shoulder at Gamadge, and asked thickly: "Is that what you were up to?"

Macloud admonished him: "I wish you'd let me get on with it. I repeat that Florence had every reason to make a new will, and without loss of time. I pass over the bequests to the servants; they are generous, and they have not been changed since I drafted the will she made three years ago. I pass over Miss Corinne Hutter's annuity, and I arrive at the specific bequests.

"First: To Mrs. Sarah Margaret Deedes, one hundred thousand dollars."

"Oh, darling, darling Florence!" Mrs. Deedes leaned back in her corner of the sofa and began to cry. Macloud, after a moment's benevolent survey of her, continued:

"Second: To Miss Suzanne Caroline Burt, one hundred thousand dollars."

Susie Burt did not speak; but her eyes turned sidewise towards Mason, and away again.

"Third: To Miss Evelyn Wing, one hundred thousand dollars, the testator's personal chattels—furniture, clothing, jewellery—and the property known as Underhill."

Evelyn Wing stood looking at him. As Gamadge had already noted, Mrs. Mason's death had changed her for the time being into a kind of automaton; the news of her legacy was powerless to break through the ice in which she seemed to be enclosed. She looked rather blankly at Macloud, and said nothing.

Mrs. Deedes's cry, "Oh, Evvie, I'm so glad!" drowned Miss Burt's short laugh. Macloud went on:

"To Timothy Mason, one hundred thousand dollars. And the residuary estate to the Bethea Home for Destitute Children, and to Florence's church in New York."

There was a dead silence. Then Mason asked in a muffled voice: "When did she cut me out, Bob?"

"Cut you out? My dear man! A hundred thousand—"

"Yes, I know." He shook his head impatiently. "Cut me out as a residuary legatee."

"I don't know at all."

"I was residuary in that will you drew up for her three years ago. Is that thing you have there legal?"

"Perfectly."

Corinne Hutter spoke with some firmness: "I think it's a very fair, nice will. I don't know why anybody should look as if they'd lost their last cent."

Percy said, with an amused glance at her: "You ought to be residuary legatee. The last of the Hutters."

"I'd just as soon not be, the way things are now."

Mason had risen. He went part way to the door, walking like an old man; stopped to say half-audibly: "Underhill," and then went on out of the room. Mrs. Deedes got up, cast an anxious look towards Evelyn Wing, and followed Mason. Susie Burt followed her. Percy, after a grave nod to Macloud, also sauntered away.

Gamadge went over to the console and picked up planchette. "I'm going to remove this thing from circulation," he remarked. "It's getting on my nerves."

Corinne Hutter, her eyes fixed on Evelyn Wing, said: "I don't know why you have to look like that."

"Of course they all think I did it." Miss Wing lifted her head to meet the bright, mouselike stare. Macloud asked: "Why should they think so?"

"She's the outsider," said Corinne. "They'll pretend they think so."

"She's not an outsider to Mrs. Deedes."

Evelyn Wing said indistinctly: "Sally doesn't know me so very well." She added: "I never dreamed that Mrs. Mason was going to leave me all that money, and I don't understand why she left me Underhill. And all the furniture and things. It looks frightful; it looks as though I'd been scheming for years. And I was down in the garden this afternoon, and somebody says something was burned there."

Corinne Hutter said: "You earned that money and all the rest of it; you held down a job for four years that nobody else could handle—Susie Burt couldn't, and I couldn't. And I don't consider Underhill much of a present in these times—you couldn't hardly give it away. As for everybody thinking you killed Cousin Sylvanus and Cousin Florence, there's one person knows you didn't, and that's the person that did kill them."

Evelyn Wing shuddered; a shudder so obviously not the result of physical chill that Gamadge was impressed by it; he had never seen one of this kind, so glibly and so often referred to, in his life before. He said: "Look here—you'd be the better for a spot of brandy."

"No, thanks. I'll go to bed."

Macloud remained in the drawing-room, no doubt to

confer with Windorp; Gamadge, Corinne Hutter, and Evelyn Wing climbed to the second floor. As they reached the head of the stairs Johnny Ridley backed out of Sylvanus Hutter's room, saluted, remarked that he was making rounds, and strode down the hall.

"Lieutenant Windorp and that Morse downstairs," said Corinne, "and Johnny Ridley patrolling the house, and a man outside; we ought to be quite safe."

"Mrs. Mason ought to have been quite safe," replied Gamadge. "There is no safety in numbers in this house, Miss Hutter; I'm quite aware of that now."

"You don't mean you think anybody else is going to be murdered, do you?" She looked at him in surprise. "Why should they be?"

"You have satisfied yourself as to the motives of this murderer, have you?"

"Well, everybody got money. Even me," she said, with her dry smile.

"The police won't bother *you* on the score of your legacy," said Gamadge. "Don't worry about that. I can swear as often as necessary that you couldn't possibly have known you were to get a penny under any of Mrs. Mason's wills."

"Well, it still *might* be a maniac," said Corinne, "so I shall lock my door. And you'd better lock yours, Evelyn, and the one to your bathroom."

Evelyn Wing had walked down the hall to her own door. They joined her as she opened it, went in, and turned on a light; it was a pleasant little oblong room, with a white-curtained window at the end of it, white woodwork, bright-patterned chintz and plain modern furniture. She said: "I'm not afraid of Susie Burt."

"You share a bath with Miss Burt?" asked Gamadge.

"Yes." She glanced at an open doorway on her right, just within the room.

"Is that a closet?" he looked at another door opposite the bath.

"Yes."

"Oblige me by looking into it."

She seemed to wonder whether he could be in earnest; then, without smiling, opened the closet door.

"Thanks," said Gamadge. "Shall I go up with you, Miss Hutter, and watch you do the same?"

"I guess nobody could hide very long in my closet," replied Corinne; "it's about a foot deep."

"You are more solicitous about others than about yourself."

"I said I'd lock my door, and I have five servants on the same floor with me—six, because the kitchenmaid is staying—and a policeman tramping past every few minutes. And I can yell out of the window."

"And Mr. Percy is next door to you," said Gamadge.

"I guess I won't bother him," said Corinne. "If he's anything like he used to be when he was younger, I'd have to throw water on him to wake him up."

Evelyn Wing said good-night, and shut them out. Gamadge went along the passage with Corinne, to meet Johnny Ridley coming back from the third floor. He looked in need of sleep.

"Aren't you going to be relieved for night duty?" asked Gamadge.

"Have to make out till six to-morrow," said Johnny. "We don't have a regiment, Mr. Gamadge—that was a funny thing, Mrs. Mason making that will, and getting it witnessed and everything, just in time."

"Yes, wasn't it?"

"Can I tell about it now? My mother'd like to hear about it. It's not the kind of thing happens every day."

"Tell anybody you want to," said Gamadge. "Why not? I dare say it'll be in all the Monday morning papers."

He bade Corinne Hutter good-night, and came back to his

room. Macloud was making himself comfortable there, and greeted his host with the remark that there was ice in the wash-basin.

"Ice?" Gamadge laid planchette down on a table and
stared.

"Louise, God bless her, put off her grief long enough to get
me some. Have you whisky? But I needn't ask."

Gamadge got a flask out of his bag, and mixed highballs.
"Windorp is dead set on Mason, assisted by Susie Burt," said
Macloud. "He thinks Mason shows all the signs of post-murder
reaction, and that Susie's capable of anything. I don't think he
was favourably impressed by the way she split on all her friends
this afternoon."

"How did she assist?" asked Gamadge.

"Typed the things in the book; Mason pretended to think
Wing had done it, and got this boomerang—the change of will."

"If I were Mason, the change of will would be quite enough
to flatten me out. Why should he have cooked up a case against
Evelyn Wing, if he still thought he was residuary legatee?"

"Afraid she'd cut him out; which of course she did."

"Miss Wing's your candidate, isn't she?"

"Well, I never did like these undue influences. I've seen too
many of 'em in my law practice. It's a brute of a case, Gamadge.
If it isn't solved all these people are pretty well ruined for life. I
wish you had something in mind."

"I have." Gamadge swallowed part of his highball. Macloud
sat up in his chair.

"You have?"

"Evidence, no; proof, no; but I think I've spotted the murderer."

"Can't you do anything?"

"I'm going to try to do something; but whether it will work,
I have no ghost of an idea."

Macloud, his saturnine gaze wandering about the room,
said that Gamadge might consult planchette for advice.

"I may, to-morrow."

"Are you daft, too? Mason seems to think that Sally Deedes has been less so than she seemed. Getting fake messages and passing them along to Florence. I hope not."

"Don't hope too much from this case, Macloud; it's a bad one."

CHAPTER FIFTEEN

Slacks

*B*EFORE GOING DOWN TO BREAKFAST on Sunday morning Gamadge, warned by sounds of activity within and without the house, looked from Sylvanus Hutter's window. He saw the cars parked in the drive, and caught a glimpse of Macloud, supported by the presence of two state policemen, glumly handing out typed statements to a ravening press. He gained the dining-room by way of the back stairs, the rear passage, and the side door.

One of the large, phlegmatic maids served him. She said that Thomas was "not so well."

"Splendid, the way you're all keeping your heads," said Gamadge, enjoying his coffee and his perfectly cooked eggs and bacon. The tall maid, soldierly and trim in her grey uniform, did not deign to reply. If she could lose her head in any circumstances, he thought, then so could the Jungfrau.

Sergeant Morse came in to say that the lieutenant wished

to see him in the library. Gamadge rose, cigarette in mouth. "You been up all night, Morse?" he mumbled.

"Lieutenant and I had shakedowns in the library."

Windorp looked none the worse for his shakedown; he was sitting at the round table, his papers spread out before him. There was a chair drawn up opposite him; no doubt it was for the accommodation of witnesses.

He said: "Good morning. The slacks in the urn were one hundred per cent wool. The article had been doused in cleaning fluid before burning, and the ashes damped down with water afterwards. Just enough smell left half an hour or so later for Beaver to notice it. No buttons or other metal fastenings were found."

"Quick work."

"My man in Bethea did it for me last night. I got the report this morning early. He found a piece under the microscope that says the stuff was probably dark blue."

"He's good."

"The murderer needed all of that forty minutes, I should say."

"And got most of them; all but two or three minutes to see Louise and myself upstairs, and two or three for safety at the other end."

Windorp frowned. "If it was Mason, he'd have had to come back to the house to change the capsules, and then get out again so as to come back from his walk later. But how could he or his accomplice know they'd have a chance to change the capsules?"

"Just luck that the chance came so soon. The death of Mrs. Mason was premeditated, the time of death not."

"I don't know why Miss Wing, or anybody, should take a walk down in that place on a cold, disagreeable afternoon. If it was Mason she saw, she ought to be able to tell him from Percy. I'll talk to her about that. Before I see these people again I want to get the Mason wills straight in my head. Mr. Macloud gave me notes on 'em." He shuffled his papers.

"Quite simple," said Gamadge. "She made one shortly after her marriage, leaving all she possessed to Mason. First fine careless rapture, you know."

"Yes; and Mason admits he knew about that one."

"We can forget that one. She made another, three years ago, leaving twenty-five thousand each to Mrs. Deedes, Miss Burt, and Miss Wing, and making her husband residuary legatee. It also gave him Underhill and her effects."

"Mason won't admit he ever saw that one, but he says he understood he was still residuary legatee in it. The other beneficiaries say they had a vague idea they were down in it for something good. But not one of 'em, and not Mason, will admit that they knew a thing about the will that was made last Thursday. Macloud says you say they may have seen drafts or copies, or the Thursday will itself."

"Or Mrs. Mason may have told Mason—or implied—that she was going to make a new will, cutting him out."

"Point is that if they did any of them know about the Thursday will, none of them but Evelyn Wing had more than a fifty thousand dollar motive for these murders. On Thursday she's made residuary legatee; on Saturday Hutter and then Mrs. Mason are killed."

"Mason still thought he was residuary legatee."

"It's in his favour that he admits it."

"Don't forget the tampering with Mrs. Mason's books, Windorp."

Windorp groaned. "Has that got to tie up with the murders?"

"Yes, it has."

"Then either Mason tried to ruin Wing with Mrs. Mason before Mrs. Mason could change the will in her favour, or Wing committed the murders before anybody could do anything else to set Mrs. Mason against her."

"The trick made her residuary legatee, no matter why it was done."

Windorp asked, scowling at Gamadge: "Who's Evelyn Wing's heir?"

"Mrs. Deedes, I fancy"

Windorp groaned again, pushed his papers aside, and summoned Morse. "Get that maid Louise in here," he said.

Louise had a swollen, tear-stained face, and red eyes; but there was a doggedness about her. She accepted Windorp's invitation to sit in the witness chair. Gamadge retired to the embrasure of one of the east windows, and stood there looking out at parked cars, great beeches, and a sullen sky.

"I'm sorry to bother you again," said Windorp. "I know how you must be feeling."

"Both gone." She looked piteously at Gamadge. "Both gone, and Underhill will belong to a stranger."

"Terrible," said Windorp.

"Who is going around killing people in ze house?"

"We're going to find out, and you're going to help us. Which of the ladies here wears slacks?"

"Slex?"

"Ladies' trousers." Windorp patted his own breeched leg.

"Oh. Madame never liked zem, she always told ladies zey looked bad in zose zings."

"She was right."

"Madame would not even wear pyjamas; just her beautiful nightdresses. She asked her friends not to wear slex at Underhill."

"But they have them, don't they, to wear other places?"

"Only Mees Wing. She has grey flannel slex, but she never wears zem here."

"Miss Hutter?"

Louise looked astonished. "Mees Corinne has no clothes, she does not dress at all."

"Certainly she wears clothes—I've seen her in 'em."

"I mean she is not *habillée*. She does not follow fashion. She would not wear slex."

"Just covers herself up with something." Windorp remained grave. "One of these ladies might have slacks, though, and you not know it."

"Not unless zey hide zem! I unpack for ladies, I look over zeir zings."

"How about the servants?"

Louise, in spite of her sorrow, could not but smile. "Zose beeg Danes? Zey would look wonderful in slex!"

"Don't wear them?"

"Never. Never in zis house have I seen anybody, anybody at all, in slex."

"Well, thank you, that's all for now. Morse, show her out, and get Miss Wing here."

When Louise had been escorted from the library Windorp turned to Gamadge. "Mason has no slacks that would go over his trousers, he said. No dungarees or overalls on the place would go on him. Nothing of the kind is missing from the garage or the stables, and Thomas says there's not an extra pair of trousers gone. He valets the men."

Gamadge said that he hoped he had not been wasting Lieutenant Windorp's time on slacks.

Evelyn Wing came in, and at a gesture of Windorp's took the witness stand. Her eyes had the glazed look that comes from a sleepless night, but she was neat and self-controlled, and her hands lay quiet on her lap.

"Who is your heir, Miss Wing?" asked Windorp.

The question seemed to amaze her. "My heir?" She collected her thoughts. "Cousin Sally, I suppose. Mrs. Deedes."

"You have no other relative?"

"No."

"Made a will?"

She shook her head.

"You have a good deal to leave, you know, since yesterday. Money, and all this." Windorp indicated the room, but seemed to include the house and property in his gesture. "All the stuff here, too," he said, and glanced up at the black-marble chimney-piece, one end of which was bare, the other decorated by a slim bronze figure leaning gently to the right. All the furniture; the chair you're sitting on, the rug under your feet, the knives and forks you eat with."

She said: "It's incredible. Mrs. Mason never meant that will to stand—never. Why should I have so much?"

"You had a lot more yesterday, or would have had if Mr. Gamadge hadn't persuaded Mrs. Mason to change her will."

"She did things on impulse. She wouldn't have let it stand."

"She wasn't given much time to change it. Now, Miss Wing; you said yesterday that you saw Mr. Percy down in that walled garden about five minutes past five o'clock. He says he wasn't there. How did you come to make such a mistake?"

"I only saw his hat."

Windorp's lower lip came out as he sat back to glare at her. "You only saw—you didn't tell us so at the time."

"Because I assumed that it was Mr. Percy. I saw his hat moving along behind a hedge, and I thought of course that he was wearing it."

"You know his hat, do you?"

"Yes."

"Where exactly was it when you saw it moving along?"

"Behind the outer hedge, going towards the south. The east hedge. I was on the west side of the pool."

"On the level part of the place, or on the steps, or down beside the pool itself?"

"I don't quite remember; but I only saw a hat."

"You must remember. Anybody would remember a thing like that."

"I really don't."

"I suppose you realize that if you were up on the ground

level you would have seen more than a hat? You would have seen a head under the hat?"

"I suppose I should have."

"You know where you were standing, Miss Wing. You won't be able to get away with that story on oath."

"I only saw a hat."

"That's what you say now, when you know that instead of its being an alibi for Percy it's the other thing. Where are your grey slacks?"

She started violently, recomposed herself, and replied: "In a trunk in the storeroom on the top floor."

"Trunk locked?"

"No. The woman who was here yesterday went all through our trunks and things."

"She wasn't told to look for slacks. Morse, tell Briggs to go up there and get these slacks and bring 'em down."

While they waited, Windorp sat looking at Miss Wing as a large dog looks at a cat which has placed itself just out of his reach. Morse came back, and resumed his shorthand. Windorp spoke to her slowly:

"Miss Wing, I'll make a suggestion to you. I'll say what the lawyer would say to you in court. He'd say you didn't see a hat moving along behind the east hedge, going south. He'd say you were wearing that hat yourself, and Percy's coat, and you dragged Percy into it because you were afraid somebody might have seen you going down to the walled garden. He'd say you put those quotations in Mrs. Mason's book yourself, to persuade her that Mason was trying to make trouble for you. He'd say that nobody but you said one word about that walled garden yesterday, and you mentioned it because you were afraid you might have been seen coming back, and didn't dare say nothing about it. And he'll ask you why you didn't speak to Percy—call out, say something."

"I didn't feel like talking to anybody." She was looking intently at Windorp, but he had not shaken her. She answered him calmly enough.

"You didn't smell anything burning up while you walked back to the house?"

"They're always burning leaves and things. I didn't notice."

"You'd have noticed that smell."

Officer Briggs, a blond heavyweight, came in with a pair of grey flannel slacks over his arm; Windorp asked; "These yours, Miss Wing?"

"Yes."

"The only ones you had up here?"

"Yes."

"That's all for the present."

She went slowly from the room; Windorp sent Briggs for Percy, who must have been waiting near the door of the library, for he lounged in almost before Briggs had had time to cross the hall. He immediately caught sight of the slacks, which Briggs had draped over the arm of a chair, and asked in a tone of great surprise: "What are you doing with my summer trousers?"

"Those are slacks, Mr. Percy; ladies' slacks. Could you wear 'em?"

Percy went over and picked them up. He held them against himself, cogitated, and said: "A trifle small in the waist and broad in the beam; but I could get them on; only they'd be short, you know."

"Mason?"

"Couldn't get into 'em."

"These belong to Miss Wing."

"Do they? I haven't seen them on her."

"But she wears slacks, since she bought these. Why should she have left the garden without speaking to you, Mr. Percy, if she thought she saw you in it?"

Percy hesitated, considered the question, and at last said with a semblance of great candour: "The truth is, Lieutenant

Windorp, that our relations are slightly strained. A couple of weeks ago I made honourable advances at her, and she repulsed them."

"Why?"

"She is a proud spirit, and she thinks I am frivolous, unaccountable, and light-minded."

"Thought you were Miss Burt's property, perhaps?"

"Miss Burt doesn't care a hang about me, but Miss Wing is scrupulous."

"Miss Wing thinks you always tell the truth. She thinks that if you say you weren't in the garden yesterday, she must have only seen your hat."

"If she says that, then she only did see my hat," said Percy, looking dazed.

"This is a murder investigation, so I have to ask personal questions. Have you means to support a wife?"

Percy's head turned rather stiffly on its neck to look at Gamadge, and then back again to Windorp. His voice has lost its lightness when he replied: "I don't know what you consider sufficient means to support a wife. Miss Wing has been poor; with me she would be less poor than she once was."

"Would have been, you mean, if she hadn't inherited a hundred thousand dollars and this property from Mrs. Mason."

"Let me inform you of something. Mrs. Mason loathed marriages among her young friends. They made barren her life, as Swinburne would have said, and, in fact, did say. She would not have objected to Susie Burt marrying, because she was not personally attached to Susie; but she might very well have cut Miss Evelyn Wing off with a shilling if Miss Wing had married me."

Windorp leaned back in his chair to look at Percy with some surprise. Percy, with a sudden start, looked at him; and Gamadge said gently: "Logic is a rare and priceless gift. You see what cross-examination would do to you, Mr. Percy? Lieutenant Windorp possesses that art in the highest degree."

Percy said: "I talk too much, and that's a fact."

"It was Swinburne that let you down. Lieutenant Windorp can't be confused by words, no matter how many of them there are."

Windorp, if gratified by this praise, did not show gratification; he merely said: "I don't suppose you'd repeat that statement on the witness stand, and this isn't a court of law."

"But Sergeant Morse seems to have it on the record." Percy's dark eyes were on the sergeant's shorthand pad.

"You haven't signed any statement."

"Let me qualify what I said. If I seemed to provide Miss Wing with an additional motive for committing two murders, or if I provided myself with one, it was because the notion was too preposterous to register itself properly on my brain. Mrs. Mason was not the most constant of human beings, you know; I haven't a word to say against her, I was extremely fond of her and she was always charming to me. But she tired of people. She wouldn't have gone on cherishing Miss Wing for ever. At best, she'd have turned her off at last with a small pension and her blessing. Evelyn Wing knew three years ago that she was down for something in Mrs. Mason's will—she had no reason to think that she was still down for it. With Mrs. Mason nobody could count on anything."

"Heavy going," said Windorp. "Nobody knows what Miss Wing knew about those wills; and now you tell us that she probably stood to lose what she *was* down for if she married you."

"Henceforth I shan't volunteer information."

Gamadge said: "I wonder if you'd tell *me* something."

"I doubt it very much; I don't feel inclined to tell anybody anything." Percy's eyes had a savage anger in them, and Gamadge thought he had a distinct glimpse for a moment of Glenido, a Roman Gentleman.

"I merely want to know why you didn't say anything when you realized that the books you were reading were being used to corrupt the text of Mrs. Mason's novel."

"I didn't fully realize anything of the sort until the Marlowe showed up. I didn't recognize the Poe, the Ford, or the Herbert."

"You said nothing to Sylvanus or to Mrs. Mason."

"I wasn't afraid they'd think I had a hand in it, of course; a child of six would have replaced the books after using them. But—again, I don't like to criticize Mrs. Mason."

"That's understood."

Percy looked at him quietly. "I've stayed in this house," he said, "time and again, since childhood. I told you that Mrs. Mason was always kindness itself to me. But I know the kind of atmosphere she created about her, and I have witnessed such exhibitions of jealousy, deceit and small cruelty here, such tale-bearing, injustice and general deviltry that no outbreak of childish revenge would have surprised me. That's what I thought it was, and I think so now; a mean way of getting back at Mrs. Mason."

"Two atrocious murders followed."

"You don't think much of my logic; now I don't think much of yours."

"I'm not speaking of cause and effect; the tampering with Mrs. Mason's script was the beginning of a long-planned campaign. Well, thanks, Mr. Percy."

Windorp nodded to Briggs, who opened the door. When Percy had gone, and Windorp had sent for Miss Burt, Gamadge asked to be excused.

"You're not interested in hearing her and Mrs. Deedes tell me they never wore slacks in their lives?"

"No. I'm going down to see what that walled garden looks like in the daytime."

"I'll miss you. I like hearing you tell people I've got the art of cross-examination. This isn't for the record, Morse; but I didn't know where Percy was heading for till he got there."

"Didn't you? Poor Percy."

"If he or any of them thinks I'm tougher than you are, they're making the mistake of their lives."

Gamadge, laughing, said that he was a mere jelly of sentiment. But he looked anything but sentimental as he strolled from the room, and Morse, watching him, bit the end of his pencil.

"He's got something," remarked the sergeant.

"If he has," replied Windorp, "try to shake it out of him."

"That Mrs. Deedes; you thought she was about half-crazy anyway. Perhaps she's the one ought to be locked up before she bumps the Wing girl off."

"Perhaps she wouldn't bump her off for a hundred thousand. She knows now that Wing has lost the residuary estate."

"If she had two hundred thousand and this property perhaps she thinks she'd get that husband of hers back again. I'd give money myself to see him play tennis the way he used to play it at the Bethea matches when I was a kid."

"From what I hear, you'll never see him play that or any other kind of tennis again. He's been drinking like a fish."

"He might swear off for two hundred thousand."

Windorp said: "Bring me those papers and bills out of Hutter's upstairs desk."

"Nothing there but old bills, all paid."

"I'm going to look at every paper in this house. You might as well learn it now, Morse; in a case like this, don't skip anything. We don't want to leave all the clues for that Gamadge to tell us about."

Morse got up without enthusiasm and went into the office. He came back with a discouraging mass of slips, cancelled cheques and vouchers, which he dumped on the round table. Then, sighing, he sat down opposite his superior officer. "Judson, printer," he began. "Four hundred dollars."

CHAPTER SIXTEEN

Yew Hedges

GAMADGE, STANDING ON THE BACK steps of the house, turned up the collar of his overcoat; a fitful wind was driving rags of cloud before it, and then closing them up again to shut out patches of blue. He was hailed from above, and looking up and to the left saw Corinne Hutter at her open window.

"Mr. Gamadge," she asked, "if you're going for a walk would you take the dogs? We're not allowed out and the servants are busy."

"Can't they run by themselves?"

"Oh, no; they're never out loose. Something might happen to them. A cat scratched Bobo awfully once."

"Come along yourself, and bring them."

"We're not supposed to leave the house." Gamadge hailed Briggs, who stood ten yards down the walk. "Will you be kind enough," he asked, "to see whether Lieutenant Windorp will allow Miss Hutter to go down to the walled garden with me? I'll bring her back."

Briggs went in with the message, and returned to say that Miss Hutter could go, if Gamadge would be responsible. She thereupon disappeared, the window was shut down, and Gamadge and Briggs had a smoke together.

"Don't know why all these people couldn't take a walk down here," said the officer. "I could watch in and back. Some of 'em might go crazy shut up like this; it isn't only dogs that need regular exercise."

"Humane suggestion," said Gamadge.

"These folks aren't used to being penned up. They can't all have done it."

"You weren't on hand yesterday during the catastrophes. There came to be a sort of a sense of black magic going on. Windorp can't take chances."

Corinne Hutter came out, the griffons on leashes. Her knitted cap was pulled well down over her ears, and her plaid coat buttoned to her chin. The griffons bounded in front of her, entangling themselves.

"Horrible noise they make," complained Gamadge, following along. "I think they're trying to trip you."

"They're just wild with joy at being let out; so am I, kind of. Listen to the water," she said, as they reached the mouth of the yew alley. She paused; the griffons, bounding in circles, wrapped their leashes about her skirts.

"And I bet the swimming-pool isn't any colder now than it is in August."

They entered the yew alley. She said: "I don't like these hedges. I don't like this garden at all. It was nicer when there were just trees and the stream."

"Something to be said for your point of view. Did you hear about the slacks?"

"Nobody's talking about anything else this morning."

"Hutter's murderer came this way yesterday, soon after three o'clock in the afternoon, wearing Percy's hat and coat and a pair of bloodstained slacks."

"Why did they have to be slacks?"

"It's a useful guess of mine which covers a lot of possibilities. Slacks—with all metal fastenings and buttons removed—are not so easily missed from a wardrobe as trousers or a skirt, and perhaps not so easily identified."

"They'd be pretty easily identified around here if there was anything left of them. People didn't wear slacks at Underhill."

"Perhaps people concealed slacks at Underhill; they concealed plenty of other things from Florence Mason."

A brick archway let them through into a broad walk, six feet wide and bounded on the side opposite the wall by a tall yew hedge. They went under a second arch—cut in yew—and emerged upon a large open place, bricked, and set out with flower-beds and shrubbery. A second yew hedge enclosed the inner mysteries—the dry pool, with its bronze fountain. Gamadge and Corinne Hutter descended shallow steps to the broad verge, and sat down on a stone bench. There were four of these benches, backed by flower-beds and small cedars.

"I hope you won't be cold," said Gamadge.

"I won't be if you don't stay all morning." She looked about her. "Which urn were those ashes in?"

"That one." Gamadge moved his head towards the right. "And opposite us, going along to the south, Miss Wing saw Percy's hat *passant*. If I saw such a thing I should investigate. I dislike extremely the idea of someone or something dodging about among the hedges of a place like this while I sat unaware."

Miss Hutter, slightly amused, said: "I shouldn't worry if I saw a hat."

"And how wrong you would have been yesterday, not to worry. There was a murderer—perhaps a demented murderer—under Percy's hat."

"Well, that wouldn't happen often."

"I see that you are not cursed with imagination." He added: "Perhaps I am; or did I really hear a rustling, a sound like soft footfalls on brick?"

"I guess you heard squirrels or dead leaves. Don't let them scare you." She looked at him quizzically.

"I'm so easily scared when there's a murderer loose."

"He isn't after us!"

Gamadge listened again for a moment, his hand lightly on her arm; then he said clearly: "But will be after me, when I've broadcast the fact that I know who it is."

"You do?" she looked incredulous.

"Of course I do."

"And you're going to broadcast it?"

"Well—we don't want any more fatalities, do we? Perhaps I could scare the party."

"Not just by saying so." She studied his face, trying to decide whether or not he could be serious.

"No, I need evidence. I'm going to fish for some." He removed his hand from her arm, got a pencil and an envelope out of his pocket, and wrote on his crossed knee: "Somebody behind us."

She read the message, frowned, and then nodded slightly.

He wrote: "Stay where you are," got up slowly, looked about him, slowly turned, and then sprinted up the steps and through the opening in the nearest hedge. Mrs. Deedes, bent over and motionless, craned up, saw him, and immediately fell on her knees.

"Oh, sorry," said Gamadge, assisting her to her feet and picking up her walking-stick. "Did I startle you?"

"You did, rather. I have something in my shoe. I've just been limping along, and I was trying to get it out."

Gamadge looked down at her grey sandal. "Let me help."

"It's all right now."

He put his hand through her arm and conducted her down to the bench beside the dry pool. She nodded to Corinne Hutter, who returned the nod coolly; the griffons, quietly established at Corinne's feet, gazed up at her like two disagreeable, whiskered little old men; but they did not bark.

"Cross little things," she said, smiling down at them.

"Not to you, Sally," said Gamadge.

"Oh, no; they know me." She sat beside Corinne Hutter, and Gamadge considered her; a mere bundle of nerves she was this morning, unable to look at him for more than a moment at a time, unable to be quiet. Her hands fumbled with the crook of her walking-stick, with her woollen bag, with the folds of her dress, the collar of her loose coat. She was hatless; her grey hair blew about her face.

"How did you get here?" he asked. "Did Windorp let the bars down?"

"Yes, I heard that officer—Briggs—asking Lieutenant Windorp if you and Corinne could come here, and I asked too. I hurried after you as fast as I could. I want to speak to you, Henry."

"I can go." Corinne made as if to rise, but Mrs. Deedes's gloved hand on her arm restrained her.

"No, Corinne, please stay. You're so sensible. You always liked Evelyn. Henry, she's in a dreadful state."

"Miss Wing is? Since when?"

"Ever since she came out of the library; ever since she saw Lieutenant Windorp."

"But I was there when she saw him. She seemed in pretty good shape when she left."

"She went upstairs; she wouldn't speak to me; she's locked in her room. She looked frightful. She's terrified."

"Windorp merely questioned her about that hat she saw. She seemed very shaky about it—where she was, you know."

"Why shouldn't she be? Nobody can remember just where they were standing. She had no reason to notice at the time."

"Yes, Sally, she had reason; she was looking at Percy, if her story is true, and intending to avoid him. I mean she saw Percy's hat. Windorp is naturally irritated, because he gets no clue from her as to who the person in the hat was. For instance, if she had been standing down here she could have seen Mason's hat, the top of Percy's hat, a suggestion of your hat or Miss Hutter's hat; not, I think, Miss Burt's hat at all."

"Unless," said Corinne in her driest tone, "Susie put the hat on a stick."

"Or Tim might have stooped over," said Mrs. Deedes. Gamadge and Corinne looked at her, and then at each other.

"Well," said Gamadge, "I have been indulging in macabre speculations about yew hedges; but I confess I didn't go so far as to imagine people walking along behind them like gorillas."

Mrs. Deedes ignored this. She said: "It couldn't have been Glen Percy; as he says, why should he leave his coat and hat down here under a hedge?"

Corinne fixed her round eyes on the bulging eyes of the bronze dolphin in the pool. She said: "So he could ask why he should have."

Mrs. Deedes, wide-eyed, murmured: "Oh, but that's fantastic." She went on: "It's so cruel; if poor Evelyn hadn't happened to come here for a little walk yesterday afternoon, they wouldn't keep on at her like this. There's not one atom of evidence that she knew a thing about Florence's wills; and even if she did, that's no proof—no proof—oh, it's cruel!"

"Yes, it is," said Corinne Hutter, "and I don't think they can do one thing to her; not one thing."

"She's not a bit mercenary," said Mrs. Deedes. She glanced shyly at Gamadge. "Would it—do you think I ought to advise her to give Underhill away, Henry? Would that improve her position?"

"Oh, dear," said Corinne Hutter.

Gamadge said judicially: "I don't think it would improve

her position, whatever her position may be, to begin giving her legacy away as if she were in a panic. The will hasn't been probated yet; it isn't considered at all the thing to dispose of property under a will before the will's come up for probate."

"But she can't keep Underhill going properly on the income from a hundred thousand dollars. Who knows what the income will be, if things go on as they're going? And it isn't as if she really cared about the place. What should Evelyn do with it?"

"What would you suggest her doing with it?" Gamadge looked at her gravely

"Well, I could have Bill here. He loved Underhill."

Miss Hutter emitted a faint groan. Gamadge asked: "And could you run it on the income from a hundred thousand?"

"Oh, I'd make it into a business proposition; a hospital or something, and farm the property. But Evelyn wouldn't care for that at all."

"The wind is getting pretty sharp," said Corinne, after a pause. "I guess I'll be going back to the house. I wouldn't talk to anybody else about Evelyn Wing, and Underhill, and so on, Mrs. Deedes."

"Much better to keep it off the record just now," agreed Gamadge.

Mrs. Deedes rose. "Please think of something, Henry. Please explain to Lieutenant Windorp that Evelyn wouldn't kill people. Florence and Sylvanus thought you were so good at that kind of thing." She looked at him reproachfully. He answered, still grave: "What kind of thing, Sally? Getting people out of trouble no matter what they've done?"

"You think she's guilty!" Mrs. Deedes gasped it.

"I have no evidence against anyone. I must seek guidance." He gave her a sombre smile. "Perhaps I might consult your oracle. Shall I try planchette?"

"You needn't make fun of me!"

"Certainly not; I'm quite serious."

She looked pleased, "I really think you have powers. You did get splendid results yesterday."

"Splendid; but not with planchette."

"Direct writing is supposed to be much more difficult."

"I'll have a solitary séance this afternoon in Syl's room, unless you think it wouldn't be safe for me there."

"Not safe?" she searched his face. "Why not? Poor Syl's influence ought to be very good."

"There are those African figures, you know."

She said: "Now you're really teasing me. Those things can only hurt weak people—like me." She turned away and went up the steps and across the level, walking slowly on her high heels. When she had disappeared through the arch in the hedge, and her stick no longer sounded, Corinne Hutter also rose. She disentangled the leads of the griffons, meanwhile addressing Gamadge with some hint of reproval in her voice:

"You're going to pretend to get a message from that silly planchette, and scare somebody with it; or try to."

"Not at all. People don't scare so easily. I merely wish to invite my unconscious," said Gamadge. "It responded curiously to my invitation yesterday; presented me with something I hadn't thought of for a long time. I might get a valuable hint or two from it on the present problem, if I tried."

"I must say I never thought you'd bother with a thing like that!"

"It's a form of concentration like another."

"I hope you won't concentrate on Mrs. Deedes. She's just floundering around. It doesn't mean anything."

"Let's for pity's sake keep our minds open."

At the arch in the outer wall Percy met them. He greeted them with his old airiness, or a good imitation of it: "We're all to be allowed down here without stir leashes; did you know?"

"High time," said Gamadge.

"Officer Briggs has convinced Lieutenant Windorp that one policeman can take care of it."

"Then Miss Hutter can go home alone, if she'll excuse me."

Corinne nodded, and went briskly up the yew walk, the little dogs pulling ahead. Gamadge lighted a cigarette. "Did you have a word with Mrs. Deedes on your way down?" he asked.

"If one passes Mrs. Deedes one always has a word with her, no matter how much of a hurry she or you may be in."

"I should like to bet you that she told you I was going to consult planchette this afternoon."

"Of course she did. I listened in wonder and admiration."

"I wish to plumb the depths of my unconscious."

"I wish you'd dredge up some information for me; what have they been doing to Evelyn Wing? Susie Burt found her in their bathroom, very green, taking spirits of ammonia. I think we'd better get lawyers."

Gamadge said: "I can't imagine what is troubling Miss Wing. Her control seemed very good. As Sally pointed out, or was it Miss Hutter, they have no evidence against her yet."

"Are you by any chance fool enough," asked Percy, rather roughly for him, "to read murder in that young woman's face?"

"Whose face do you read it in, Mr. Percy?"

Susie Burt came flying around the bend in the walk, called: "Tim, oh Tim," saw them, and stopped short.

"Not here yet," said Percy.

She walked past them, her head up, and vanished into the garden. After a moment footsteps sounded on the bricks. Mason came around the bend; the griffons, unleashed and at liberty, pattered meekly at his heels, stopped when he did, and sat down with their tongues out.

Mason's face, having lost its gaiety, seemed therewith to have lost all expression; it looked flattened and dull. He said dully: "Susie in there?"

"Yes," said Gamadge, "she is."

He glanced about him vaguely. "Funny, isn't it? We're all to be turned out of this place, and that Wing girl will be here. I wonder if she'd sell. She won't be able to get much for it now, and I'd offer her twenty-five thousand cash. Run it as a farm. Build breeding stables. When I think of the time and trouble I put into the property—and my own money, too!"

The others were silent. He went on, glancing at Gamadge and then away: "I know I've been a fool. I know Florence was getting tired of it, but I meant to settle down—make it up to her. I was fond of her, and she of me; we'd have patched things up, she never would have let those wills stand. Why should I have killed her?"

"Who says you killed her, Mason?"

"He says I was in love with Susie, and wanted to marry her. He says I thought I still had the residuary estate." Mason's eyes rested on Percy, and flickered past him. "Even a policeman ought to know that you're not in love with every woman you take out to dinner. It was that damned stuff somebody put into Florence's novel that dished me; decided Florence to cut me out. I say it was done to cut me out, and get the residuary estate into the open market. First come, first served. Somebody's feeling pretty silly now."

"Doesn't Miss Burt explain to Windorp that you were not in love with her?"

"She swears it. She swears she was in love with Percy but that they couldn't marry because they had no money. That puts her in a spot, and then she begins to cry. Well, she wanted to talk to me, and here I am." He brushed past them; the griffons rose sedately, and followed in single file.

Gamadge said: "Those animals behave as if they were under a spell."

"The pups? Oh, they adore Mason. He brought them up. He has a way with dogs and horses."

They walked together up the yew alley. Percy went on:

"Somebody ought to explain to Windorp that characters like Susie Burt don't commit murders; people commit murders for them, and then wish they hadn't. Mason was very much pleased a short time ago at having as he thought cut me out with Susie. I feel rather sorry for him."

CHAPTER SEVENTEEN

Evidence

GAMADGE AND PERCY EXCHANGED greeting with Officer Briggs and went into the house; Percy to walk on down the back hall and through the swing door, Gamadge to pause at the sound of Louise's voice, raised in angry complaint, issuing from the servants' sitting-room. He turned right and followed the transverse corridor until he found himself between the kitchen and the sitting-room doorways. The former was filled by a craggy form in white, its arms stretched out and its hands against either side of the door-frame. Under its right arm a freckled face—that of the local kitchenmaid—peered curiously forth.

Two equally rocklike figures, the tall blonde housemaids, stood within the sitting-room door; they watched the distracted flittings of Louise, who pattered from end to end of the large, pleasant room, gabbling nervously.

"Zey were here on the hook," she protested. "Two hours ago zey were here. Now one of zem is gone. Where is it?"

"Where is what?" asked Gamadge, and the Danes turned their heads calmly to look at him.

"Bobo's leash."

"Corinne Hutter brought them back and hung them up just a little while ago," piped the local. "I saw her." She added: "And then I went back to the potatoes."

"You should not have left the potatoes," said the craggy cook, not unamiably.

"Miss Hutter and I walked the dogs in the garden," said Gamadge, "and she must have got back not more than ten minutes ago. Fifteen at the very most."

"And in zose minutes," shrilled Louise, "Bobo's leash has gone."

The three Danes refused to care; they had not been in their sitting-room since breakfast. "And don't get eggcited," advised the cook. "It's notting to get eggcited about in this house to-day."

Gamadge, if for another reason, seemed to share Louise's perturbation. He looked apprehensive, and put two fingers inside his collar as if it had suddenly begun to feel tight on him. "Mason is walking the dogs again," he said. "They haven't leashes on, but perhaps he has one in his pocket. I suppose none of you saw anybody in the passage after this lady saw Miss Hutter come back?"

Five heads moved slowly from side to side; the local, who could not have been more than fifteen, looked highly amused at Gamadge's civil reference to her.

"Well," he said, "at least let me take the opportunity to say again how splendid I think you all are to carry right on like this. We're most grateful."

The cook said: "Least ve could do, our nice money Mrs. Mason left us in her vill."

"Momma didn't want me to stay," chirped the local, "but Corinne Hutter called her on the telephone, and I slep' with Mrs. Svensen."

"Nobody want to kill *you*," said the cook, looking down at her with benevolent derision.

"I didn't get any money in Mrs. Mason's will," said the local.

"You ought to have something; I'll ask Mr. Macloud if the estate won't give you a present," said Gamadge. "How's Thomas?"

Louise said that Thomas wasn't at all well, had had chills in the night, and was unable to leave his suite. He had a bedroom and bath of his own on the top floor.

"Has he seen a doctor?"

Louise said that Dr. Burbage was coming. "When shall we be able to get back to New York, sir?" asked the slimmer of the Danes. "I have my car; I would drive Mrs. Svensen and Greta."

"Lieutenant Windorp will give you the word. Just hang on till the party breaks up."

Gamadge strolled thoughtfully out of the kitchen precincts, and up to his room. He found Macloud in their communicating bath, putting things into his bag.

"Thought I'd save time," said the lawyer, as he tossed small articles upon one another. "I've got to keep to schedule. How about you?"

"I must."

"If you can leave by six I'll drive you down."

"If I don't finish by six I'll never finish at all. I'm consulting planchette after lunch. May I use Syl's room for the sitting?"

Macloud, sponge-case in hand, turned to stare at him. "What in the name of nonsense are you up to now?"

"Mrs. Deedes heard me say that I know who the murderer is. She'll spread it. I thought the party might want a chat with me."

"Never heard anything so idiotic in my life. You asking to get killed?"

"It's extremely hard to kill anybody who's expecting to be."

"Not with a gun."

"There'll be no gun, and no noise. Don't forget that we have a patrol. I'm rather expecting to be garrotted!"

Macloud said: "Look here. I'd better be in the offing."

"Your job is to keep the coast clear for me as well as you can by staying downstairs, and engaging Windorp in conversation. No lurking, remember; our friend isn't going to let people spring out on him or her from closets."

"I bet nothing happens. You idiot, Clara would like this!" Macloud referred to Gamadge's wife.

"She'll never hear of it. Will you stay downstairs and talk to Morse and Windorp?" Macloud, observing that he would rather be in a cage of rattlesnakes than in this house, jammed the sponge-bag into his valise. Gamadge, leaning against the wall, said in a colourless tone: "Good deal depends on catching out this murderer. Money. Doesn't that appeal to you?"

"All right, all right. Silly, childish trick. Wash my hands of it." Macloud nearly sent the valise off the bathroom stool to the floor. A new trooper, announcing himself as Officer Poultney, came in to say that Lieutenant Windorp wanted to see Mr. Gamadge and Mr. Macloud right away.

"Hope this means Windorp has real evidence," grumbled Macloud, on their way downstairs. "If not, think I'll turn informer."

Gamadge said a little awkwardly: "I don't want to be sentimental; but perhaps you'll agree with me that I owe Florence something."

"Not your life," growled Macloud.

"Just a slight risk."

Macloud said no more. Officer Poultney had preceded them to the library; he shut them into it and withdrew, leaving them to confront a Sergeant Morse whose expression was one of subdued triumph, and a Lieutenant Windorp who sat regarding them with a kind of grudging satisfaction.

"Well, Mr. Gamadge," he said, "I hand it to you."

"Hand what to me?"

"This." Windorp held out a small, oblong slip of greyish paper. It was scrawled with hieroglyphics in blue crayon, through which printed matter was discernible. Gamadge took it, looked at it, and passed it to his friend.

It was a cash sales slip, recording the purchase of one pair of navy-blue slacks at a large department store in New York. On the back of it was pencilled: "Miss E. Wing. To be called for."

"And where do you think we found it?" Windorp was grinning from ear to ear. "Among Sylvanus Hutter's old bills and cancelled cheques. She was working on 'em last Fall, and this got mixed in. How does it feel to have your notions come true?"

Gamadge took the slip back from Macloud and examined it.

"You're thorough, Windorp."

"Routine."

"I owe you a piece of corroborative evidence. Miss Wing came into Hutter's room last night just before dinner. She didn't expect to find me there; I think she was going to look for this in Syl's desk."

"She never had a chance. We cleared the desk out first thing."

"So I intimated to her. I don't know," said Gamadge, looking at the pencilled notation on the back of the slip, "why a customer's name should be written on a sales slip for a cash purchase."

"We'll ask her. Morse, get her in here." He turned to Macloud. "Thought you'd be willing to sit in on this as a neutral observer. Keep the record straight, so Miss Wing won't be able to plead coercion or anything."

"I can't act for her, Windorp; I represent the other side—the Hutter-Mason estate."

"You don't mind standing by?"

"Not at all, if you won't mind my butting in, when and if it seems expedient."

"Butt in all you want to."

Macloud went to a chair on the other side of the fireplace; Gamadge once more retired to the window embrasure.

"I dare say you'd like to arrest her on the strength of this?" Macloud, crossing his legs, leaned back in his chair and pointed to the sales slip, now in Windorp's fingers again.

"I dare say I would; but we'll give her a chance to explain."

"She can't very well explain away her having lied about the possession of other slacks."

"That's what I thought."

"If you try to connect that slip with the ashes in the urn, though, you'll have a fight on your hands, starting in the coroner's court. A jury may try to draw an inference, but they'll be charged not to draw it. We don't know that the ashes in that urn ever were slacks."

"There's such a thing as an overwhelming probability."

"Slacks were originally nothing but an emanation of my friend Gamadge's ever-fertile brain; there's a gap a mile wide between his theory that slacks were burned in the garden yesterday, and the slacks that Miss Wing bought in September."

Windorp's satisfaction at seeing navy-blue slacks all but materialize as a result of Gamadge's incantation, survived this legal quibbling. He said: "Let the jury hear about those ashes being wool, probably navy-blue wool—"

"And matters will proceed as I say. You didn't even find the slip while seeking confirmation of the slacks theory."

Gamadge, a shoulder propped against the window embrasure, looked out of the window. He said without turning his head: "Put off the arrest, Windorp; put it off a few hours. I may be able to dig up something better for you."

"I wouldn't put it past you to dig up anything; but she may be dangerous."

"She has her money, all she can expect now; why should she be dangerous?" asked Gamadge, while Macloud glowered at him.

"She may be partly crazy."

"Miss Wing is sane enough. Give her the run of the second floor, Windorp, until I have a try at new evidence." He added: "You have your patrol working."

Windorp looked down at the sales slip. "With this in evidence she ought to be locked up."

"Just a few hours."

"That'll give me time to look up a lawyer for her," said Macloud. "I don't know much about Bethea talent. Perhaps I ought to find somebody in New York."

Gamadge, looking out at the grey-and-blue mottled sky, did not hear Miss Wing brought in; but the timbre of her voice made him turn and look at her. It was a younger, higher voice than he had heard from her before, and her face was younger; all its maturity, its self-possession, had been washed away by a fear come true. She sat passive, almost childlike, in front of Windorp, and said: "I can explain it."

"Wish you would. Sergeant Morse here will take notes of what you say, and it might be used in evidence; so you have your choice of talking or not talking. But I hope you'll talk."

"I'd rather explain now. I got the slacks at a bargain sale in September, but I couldn't wear them here; I got them to wear next summer when I went on my vacation. Mrs. Mason didn't like me or anybody to wear slacks, and I didn't want to upset her; so I said nothing about them to her or anybody. I left them in their package in my closet. I never thought of them again until you asked me about slacks. I went and looked, and they were gone."

"Somebody took them?"

"Yes; I don't know who could have known about them."

"You bought 'em for cash?"

"Yes."

"Why is your name on the back of the slip, then?"

"I left them to be picked up, and went and did some other shopping. The girl wrote my name down so that I shouldn't have to wait if she wasn't at the counter when I got back."

"And you did Mr. Hutter's accounts, in October, I think, and mixed up this sales slip with them?"

"Yes." If she could be paler, she was now.

"You never thought of the slacks until after we talked about them a little while ago. Then why were you looking for this sales slip in Hutter's room last evening, a short time after the ashes were found in the garden?"

She said after a pause: "I'm sorry. I did begin to worry about the slacks, then. Somebody told me they were looking for slacks, and that they thought the ashes in the garden…" she stopped. Unable to go on, for the moment, Gamadge thought.

"Who told you?"

"It had got around."

"Not unless Percy spread it. Did he tell you? Rush right up to your room and tell you they'd found the ashes of your slacks?"

"He didn't rush up. He stopped and told me."

"Why couldn't you admit that at first? Why did you try to conceal it?"

"I dragged him in before."

"Oh, yes; the hat. Percy knew you wore slacks on your vacations?"

"He may have heard me say so."

"So instead of coming to me about these missing slacks of yours, you wait till you're questioned about them, and then you have a direct falsehood ready; that you had no other slacks up here but the grey ones."

"I thought it would look so badly—my having concealed them."

"And when the sales slip is found you tell another falsehood;

that you didn't think about it until this morning. I could hold you on a charge of obstructing justice; and I think if Mr. Gamadge hadn't been in Hutter's room last evening you would have made yourself liable to another charge—destroying evidence."

She turned her pale, blank face aside. "I'd been down in the garden. I was too frightened to tell the truth."

"Then what part of your evidence do you expect us to believe? What part of it is likely to be believed in a court of law? Why should we believe you didn't know that Mrs. Mason had you down in that will she made Thursday, as her residuary legatee?"

She was silent.

"You want us to think that somebody poked around in your closet sometime and found your blue slacks. Who was likely to do that? The servants?"

"Oh, no, they wouldn't."

"That Louise wouldn't? One of my men says she was digging in your closet yesterday, after you went down to dinner."

Gamadge said: "Mrs. Mason sent her to get clothes for Miss Hutter to wear. A dressing-gown, and so on."

"Thanks." Windorp was brusque with his tame magician. "Does she often do that? Prowl in your room?"

"Never. She's incapable of it."

"We don't know what people are capable of, though, do we?" Gamadge thought that Windorp had been too modest in disclaiming powers of cross-examination. "Somebody looked for slacks in your closet," he went on. "Knew where to look, too. Wore them to kill Hutter, got bloodstains on them, and wore them down to the garden. Burned 'em in that urn, with cleaning fluid poured over 'em; and left Percy's hat and coat there under a hedge. You were there, by your own account you left the garden just on the minute—just in time to miss the bonfire. You won't tell us where you were standing when you saw Percy's hat. How do you think that adds up, Miss Wing?"

She said: "I can't add it up. I've told you everything, now."

"I'm giving you a chance to say who knew about your navy-blue slacks. You must have told somebody about them."

"No, I didn't."

"Nobody'd hunt in your closet just for the fun of it."

There was a pause, and then she looked not at Macloud but at Gamadge. "Can they arrest me?"

He said: "Ask Mr. Macloud."

Macloud said: "They would be justified, I think, in holding you for questioning. If they do, I'll get you a lawyer—anybody you want, or you can leave it to me. To be frank, I think they have a prima-facie case against you; but my line isn't criminal law. You'd better have expert advice."

"I'll let Miss Wing think it over for a while," said Windorp, after a visible struggle with himself. "That's all for now."

She rose; turning an incredulous, pale stare on him, she asked slowly: "You're not arresting me?"

"No. You're free, Miss Wing," said Windorp drily, "as air; except I don't care to have you leave the house. But so far as I know you don't want to; you didn't ask permission to go and take a walk in the garden this morning, though everybody else did." He added, over his shoulder, "And you needn't put that down, Sergeant Morse; perhaps the lawyers would call that immaterial."

"But not irrelevant," murmured Macloud, as she went out of the room.

Windorp leaned back, his hands clasped behind his head. "My idea is that she wore those slacks and committed the first murder. She was the one that had the best opportunity to go through Mrs. Mason's papers, and Hutter's too; it was her job. Of course she read all the drafts of all the wills, soon as they were put in Mrs. Mason's desk. She came back to the house, waited around for a chance, and changed those capsules—she'd have known all about Hutter's photography and his chemicals. It's a clear case of a penniless woman, in love with a poor man; and now she's started behaving the way she's going to behave in the courtroom—young and helpless; and both of you fell for it. I wish people would ever think of the victims in a murder case."

Macloud, with his eyes on Gamadge, said that he didn't know why Windorp was attacking them in this manner.

"Because I'm sore at the way this thing is bound to go. She has her story, and unless Mr. Gamadge digs up something more it'll get her off."

Macloud said: "If it hadn't been for Gamadge she would never have had to tell it."

"That's why I've turned her loose for the afternoon. If it hadn't been for Mr. Gamadge," said Windorp, putting his forefinger on the sales slip, "we'd never have looked twice at this thing. I'm glad to oblige him; but I'm not very calm in my mind about her; now's the time for her to plant evidence on somebody else."

"What has she to plant?" asked Gamadge.

"Couple of pinches of cyanide crystals."

"If she's the murderer," said Gamadge, "she won't plant them on anybody."

"How do you know?"

"There isn't a person in the group," said Gamadge, "who wouldn't take cyanide rather than go to the electric chair."

"Well, you're responsible for her, don't forget that." The luncheon gong sounded as he rose. "Morally responsible," he added dourly. "But if she kills somebody else, or herself, you won't be blamed; I will."

CHAPTER EIGHTEEN

End of Planchette

CORINNE HUTTER HAD NOT ONLY KEPT order in the pantry and kitchen, she had actually argued or persuaded the entire party at Underhill into coming to lunch. They drifted, one after the other, into the white and mirrored dining-room, and Corinne took charge of them; if she had not, Gamadge thought, they would probably have drifted away again. Corinne, as she placed them, had a firm hold on Mason's arm.

"Cousin Tim," she said, "you sit in Cousin Florence's place, and Mr. Macloud can sit opposite you. Greta, isn't Lieutenant Windorp going to eat with us?"

This question showed less than her usual dry tact; unless she had asked it in the sure and certain knowledge that he wasn't, and merely to show that nobody, so far as she could guess, needed to be afraid of the law

"He's going to have a tray in the library," said Greta, the biggest parlourmaid.

"Then let's sit down."

Corinne Hutter could make them sit down, but she could not make even Percy talk; and she could not make Evelyn Wing eat. It was Macloud who took over, much to Gamadge's admiration. He began immediately to discourse on the laws of the Saxons, kept up his lecture through the first two courses, and had reached (by some process Gamadge could not follow) a disquisition on English court procedure under James I by the time they were finishing the squabs.

By this strategy he had driven Mason to begin a low-voiced conversation about air defence with Mrs. Deedes; and Percy, without much spirit, was explaining to Evelyn Wing—who took no notice of him—that he had had a prejudice against Germany ever since he had seen a certain worm at the Falls of the Rhine; which he declared to have been the size and colour of a small cooked lobster, and covered with black spots.

Coffee was served at table. When it had been swallowed Mason excused himself, and disappeared through the side door. The others melted away, and Macloud, Gamadge, and Corinne Hutter were left standing together, looking relaxed.

"You're a genius, Corinne," said Macloud.

"Well, if I am, you're a hero. I thought it was perfectly terrible for Cousin Tim to keep going without his meals, and if he could come down the others certainly ought to be able to stand it. People have to eat."

"You certainly cast a spell over the servants. I thought they'd have been in a huddle by now," said Gamadge, "with two policemen taking care of them."

"Mr. Macloud helped me. He went right up yesterday and told them about their legacies, and said he'd get their wages paid for six weeks if they'd stay till we didn't need them."

"No difficulty at all," said Macloud. "The cook was sitting on her packed trunk, and I helped her unpack it again."

"I ought to see about a caretaker. Will you talk to the stableman that always did it, Mr. Macloud? I don't know what to tell people about their wages. I don't know exactly who the place belongs to right now. Can Evelyn Wing give orders about it? Cousin Tim won't; he won't settle a thing. He seems to think he hasn't any right even to sleep here one night."

"He has to," said Macloud, "until Windorp breaks up the party. I'll see the men."

"Evelyn Wing—she looks as if she'd had a sickness. Is—I hope nothing's going to happen to her?"

"Don't worry about it," said Macloud. "Go ahead with your own job. I suppose you wouldn't care to stay on and look after the place for the time being? I can get you appointed for the estate until things are settled."

"You wouldn't say that unless Evelyn Wing—this is terrible."

"Of course it's terrible. The whole thing is terrible," said Macloud, irritated.

"I have to be at the library to-morrow morning, if Lieutenant Windorp will let me; but I could drive back and forth for a while. Doctor Burbage thinks Thomas ought to go to the hospital, or he might have a stroke. It's been too much for him."

"I'll talk to Burbage on the telephone this afternoon."

Gamadge left them discussing ways and means, and walked through the deserted drawing-room. Florence and Sylvanus had made it, and without them it seemed already to be fading; but the Danes had made up the fire and filled the vases with fresh hothouse flowers—the blight, if there were one, could not be any fault of theirs.

Much depressed, he walked slowly up to the second floor, and could have embraced Officer Poultney when the latter advanced towards him from the rear of the hall. "You're alive, anyway," said Gamadge. "I salute you."

"It is kind of dead up here, isn't it?" Poultney glanced over his shoulder. "They all shut themselves up soon as they came upstairs. All these doors, I'm getting to hate the sight of them. That linen closet there—last time I looked in, a big roll of blackout stuff fell off a shelf on me."

"In your place I should have screamed aloud."

"I might've if I hadn't been in uniform."

Poultney went on down the stairs, and Gamadge was about to open his door when the griffons dashed around the corner from the back passage, to fling themselves upon him, wheezing.

"Why, you poor little beggars," Gamadge looked down at them with some sympathy. "Lonely, are you? Looking for Florence and Syl? No, you can't come in with me—I'm busy."

But they could and did. They rushed through his room and into the communicating bath; a squeal and a clatter brought Gamadge after them, to find that Bobo, trying for a short cut into Hutter's room, had brought Macloud's valise down from the bath stool and himself sprawling on the tiles. Dodo, concerned for her partner, stood panting.

Bobo was not hurt. Gamadge shooed both animals into the hall, closed his door, and possessed himself of a couple of sheets of notepaper and planchette. Then he went into the bathroom and inspected the damage. There was not much. None of the bottles and small toilet articles which strewed the floor was broken, but a tin of superior talcum had lost its top and shed part of its contents on the tiles. He fanned powder to right and left, replaced the things in the valise and the valise on the stool, and went through into the next room, shutting the door after him.

He arranged the paper and planchette on a small table, lowered the blinds, drew the curtains, and placed a chair at the table with its back to the bathroom. Then he sat down and poised his fingers on the board.

Almost immediately he felt a fullness in his head. Funny, he thought, it was my hands yesterday; and wondered afresh at the effect of ritual on mankind. "And what you fellows don't know about that!" he muttered, raising his eyes to the little black misshapen figures on the mantelpiece.

The hall door opened. Evelyn Wing came in, closing it behind her, at the same moment that Gamadge heard the heavy steps of the patrol in the upper hall.

Gamadge, frowning heavily, shook his head, made a face at her, and formed silent words: "Go away."

She moved forward instead, put another chair opposite him, and sat down on it. "Had to speak to you," she said, below her breath.

"No. Later. Can't listen now." He pushed planchette about the paper, and then pointed. She read in large block letters what he had written upside down: "Go now."

She looked at him, and down at the board. She seemed to be asking herself whether he could really be taking this mumbo-jumbo seriously, whether she ought to revise her opinion of him after all. Her face, seen as an almost expressionless mask in the gloom, told him nothing; but as she in turn put her hands on planchette, her head came up, and she was suddenly rigid. Gamadge also had heard the faint, very faint, click of a lock—the lock belonging to the hall door. He smiled at her.

She wrote, slowly and painfully, as if with frozen fingers. He read her message: LOOK OUT.

"Thanks," he murmured, still smiling, and they sat gazing at each other, poised, tense, waiting.

There was a change in the room, impalpable as air; in fact, it might have been air that caused it—the faintest draught. Gamadge rested his chin on his hand; Miss Wing stared beyond his shoulder; and suddenly she rose. Gamadge put out a hand to seize her wrist, but she had gasped:

"The bathroom door!"

He swung out of his chair sidewise, and his elbow swept planchette from the table. He reached the bathroom door as if catapulted against it, but the latch had clicked, and the bolt shot home.

"Well." He stood for a moment looking at it, and then turned to look at her. "Something of an anti-climax," he said. "You have spoiled my experiment, Miss Wing, and done yourself no good. And I'm not grateful for your kind solicitude." Walking past her, he pulled back the curtains and drew up the blinds. "And I really think," he said, coming back to look down at the splintered remains of planchette, which he seemed to have put his foot on, "that the only satisfactory part of the entire transaction is this."

She had sunk back upon her chair. "You mean you were *expecting*—"

"My poor dear Miss Wing. I was expecting evidence that was to save you from the county jail. Now to jail you will probably go; and I hoped you wouldn't even have to undergo the ignominy of an arrest." He picked planchette up from the floor, and tossed its halves into a waste-basket. "Perhaps, though, you will now tell me whom *you* were expecting when the bathroom door opened."

"I just heard the latch, and saw it come ajar."

"And do you think I didn't hear the latch? I've been waiting patiently to hear it."

"I didn't come to warn you of anything. I came to ask you whether they'll just go on now and—and convict me, without ever doing anything more to find out who really killed Mrs. Mason and Mr. Hutter."

"As soon as you're arrested the entire country will begin to try and find out who really committed the murders. As soon as anybody is arrested the entire population—with a few hard-headed exceptions—decides that that party must be innocent. Don't ask me why."

"But will the police stop looking?"

"Why should they waste time and the taxpayers' money try-

ing to help a person who won't help herself?" He stood looking
down at her.

"I can't be sure."

"You want somebody else to do the dirty work? Well, if the
worst happens, I'll write you an epitaph: 'When I am dead, my
dearest, O do not Ouija me.' Apologies to Christina Rossetti."

She said in an agonized voice: "I can't do it! I don't know
anything! I don't believe it's true."

"You might consult me; I am famous for keeping harmless
secrets."

She shook her head.

"Very well, then, let us put our minds on the immediate
problem of getting ourselves out of this without a stain on our
characters. Do I hear the footsteps of Officer Poultney?"

When the footsteps came abreast of the door Gamadge
knocked on it. A key turned, and Poultney's surprised face confronted him.

"Thanks," said Gamadge. "A vulgar joke, perpetrated no
doubt by my friend Macloud."

"Mr. Macloud locked you and her in here?" Poultney
seemed incredulous.

"These reserved characters, you never know where they're
going to break out."

He and Poultney watched Miss Wing go down the hall and
into her room. When its door closed, Gamadge continued: "We
were playing planchette, but it was a stormy session, and the
medium ended by being dashed from the table to the floor. All
right, Poultney; and thanks again."

Poultney went down the front stairs. Gamadge, frowning
dejectedly, entered his own room. Afterwards he tried to remember how many seconds it was before, on his way to the communicating bath to unlock its farther door, he stopped short,
gaped, uttered a sound resembling a bellow, and turned to make
for the hall. But although he had doubts about that short inter-

val, he had no doubts as to what went through his mind as he ran shouting to Miss Wing's room. He was thundering on the panels of her door when Poultney, gun in hand, lumbered up beside him. Poultney was a man of action; he put the gun away and rammed his foot against the wood over the knob.

Morse and Windorp, pistols out, came running up. Mason, looking bewildered and half awake, peered from his room opposite; Corinne Hutter arrived from the back passage; Susie Burt put her head out of her room, and Mrs. Deedes came towards them shrieking: "What is it? What is it?" Percy had materialized from the back passage, and Macloud from the first floor by the time Poultney had kicked the door in and followed it, stumbling.

Windorp and Gamadge were behind him, and again Morse was barring the crowd out with stretched arms. He shut the door on it, and then turned to face—as the others did—an empty, quiet room. Windorp, moving his head from side to side like a frustrated buffalo, gazed at the unruffled bed, the neatly placed furniture, the orderly dressing-table. He glared at Poultney. Poultney, staggered by this tame ending to pandemonium, could only mutter:

"Mr. Gamadge told me to bust the door."

Morse was trying to fit the burst door into its frame. Gamadge lurched past him to the closet. "If this is locked," he began, but the knob turned. Gamadge, falling back as the door jerked open, did not see the huddled figure lying among bags and boxes in the dark.

And when Poultney had got it on the bed, Gamadge could only see the broad backs of the two policemen. He stood breathing hard, until Windorp turned to him with something thin and snaky in his hand. "Dog's leash," he said, panting, too.

"Yes. It's been missing."

"She's alive." Poultney spoke over his shoulder. "Needs air."

Windorp crossed the room and flung up the window. "Go to it," he said. "You're the first-aid man."

"Might send for the doc, though."

Officer Beaver had come to the door, and was exchanging whispers with Morse. He was sent to telephone, and Windorp came back to Gamadge with the leash in his hand.

"Perfect noose," he said, "with the snap end run through the thong. I don't know why her neck wasn't broken."

"Somebody in a bad hurry," said Gamadge. "Cut it pretty fine. Miss Wing left me about four minutes ago—that right, Poultney?"

"About right, sir."

"Murderer was waiting in the closet, caught her from behind as she came along the room. She'd have died in that closet."

"Yes. You saved this one." Windorp's eyes questioned him fiercely. "What gave you the idea?"

"I nearly missed it. What I was saying—the murderer had about three minutes to do the trick and get out of this; had to wait until I was in my room, and watch the hall; and I wasn't in my room more than a quarter of a minute before I came back down here."

"A quarter of a minute is plenty of time to get from one room to another. What brought you here, I'm asking you?"

"My brain actually started working, and it went on working. It's all right, I think, Windorp."

"All right? We've started all over again. This Wing girl knew something, or she wouldn't have been assaulted with intent to kill; but who assaulted her? Who's the killer?"

"Miss Wing won't be able to tell you that; I don't suppose she has any idea who it was. But as you say," he added, a faint smile on his lips, "she's out of it now."

Poultney straightened. "Breathin' quite natural. Looks bad, but she'll be all right except for shock." He pulled a quilt up over his patient.

"You're to stand by in here," said Windorp, "and not let a soul through the door till the doctor comes."

"Miss Wing ought to have a woman with her when she comes to," suggested Gamadge. "How about one of those maids? They'll look out for her and ask no questions; won't turn a hair."

"Greta Boyesen's all right," said Morse. "She's been coming up with the family years."

"Tell Beaver to get her, then."

Morse looked out into the hall. A voice which Gamadge had difficulty in recognizing as Percy's, shouted something. Morse raised his own voice, Beaver's replied, and the door was pushed to again.

"I'll stay on the job here," said Gamadge, "if you'll let Poultney and Morse and Beaver do a job for me."

Windorp growled: "What job?"

"Er—closing in on the murderer. I want a man posted at the head of the stairs, and one at this end of the hall; and I want nobody on this floor at all from now on. I want Percy, and Mason, and all the rest of them taken down to the drawing-room and kept there."

"How long?" Windorp pushed out his lower lip.

"Till Miss Boyesen relieves me, and I can come down and tell you who the murderer is. But I won't budge until everybody's in the drawing-room, and the two guards posted here, one at each end of the hall. You can spare Beaver from outside, Windorp; you don't need anybody outside from now on."

Windorp asked in a controlled voice: "You mean that—about telling who the murderer is?"

"And giving you the necessary evidence. Yes, I do." Windorp looked long at Gamadge, who returned his gaze with one that seemed to convince the lieutenant of state police. "All right," he said at last. "Out of here, you two. Morse, I'll want you to get the people downstairs. Poultney, you stay at this end of the hall; Beaver can take the other end. Stop anybody coming up or down. That right, Gamadge?"

"That's right." He added, as Beaver moved away and he caught sight of the deathly and unconscious face on the pillow, "But are you sure she's going to be all right?"

"Unless she collapses later from shock, and I don't see any sign of it; her heart's as strong as mine is."

Again, as the three officers went from the room, the inarticulate clamour arose in the hall. Words formed themselves: "You fool, I will see her! You won't say anything—I don't know whether she's dead or alive!"

CHAPTER NINETEEN

Mania

MISS GRETA BOYESEN, INSTRUCTED by Officer Poultney, came into the room, bowed politely to Gamadge, and sat down in a chair beside the bed. She looked at Evelyn Wing with the expression, detached but co-operative, of one asked to lend a hand in an emergency to a job not his own.

"Very kind of you," said Gamadge.

"The doctor is coming. Officer Poultney says I do not have to do anything."

"Except tell Miss Wing she'll be all right, and that the situation is under control; if she wakes up, you know."

Gamadge, with a last anxious look behind him, departed, wondering through what failure of intelligence or fortune Miss Boyesen was not a trained nurse. Poultney and Beaver were at their stations, the length of the dusky hall between them; he passed Beaver, went down the stairs, and entered the drawing-room.

Windorp had placed Sergeant Morse in the dining-room archway, and had lined up the party, as for official inspection, on the sofa, and a settee. They faced the east windows; Corinne Hutter, Mason, Mrs. Deedes, and Susie Burt, with Percy at the extreme right of the line, half turned from them all. He sat with his arm and hand hanging over the end of the sofa, looking out of the side window nearest him—perfectly controlled now and sombre. Perhaps he had heard that the doctor was coming, and had had his racking doubt settled for him at last. Macloud, on the piano bench far to the rear, leaned back with his arms outstretched along the closed lid. Gamadge had seen him look like that in a court-room, while awaiting the return of a jury with their verdict.

"Here's Mr. Gamadge," said Windorp, who stood with his back to the windows, facing his audience. "We'll hear what he has to say. If I did as I feel, I'd have every one of you locked up until Miss Wing was able to talk—if she ever is able. But she'd be dead and gone now if it wasn't for him, so I guess we'll let him tell how he got the idea where she was and what had happened to her."

Gamadge seemed to prefer to talk sitting down. He looked about him, pulled a straight-backed chair, the first he saw, towards the left-hand end of the line, and sat down half facing it. He crossed his knees and leaned forward, supported by an elbow.

"This case," he said, "revolves about the character and personality of Miss Evelyn Wing; a proud spirit, as Mr. Percy describes her, forced by necessity to sacrifice that pride and many other things of value to her. I dare say she often felt that in small matters she was sacrificing her self-respect; but that it could do no great harm to humour the whims of poor Florence Mason.

"I was impressed by the fact that there has been no attempt by anyone to implicate Miss Wing in the murders of Sylvanus

Hutter and Mrs. Mason. What evidence there happens to be against her was provided by herself; her walk in the garden yesterday, her loss of a sales slip which proves that she purchased navy-blue slacks."

Percy's fingers moved a little; Mrs. Deedes drew a gasping breath.

"As for the accusation that she had tampered with Mrs. Mason's novel," continued Gamadge, "that brings us to the first of the paradoxes in this most curious case. An attempt to discredit her results in her being made Florence Mason's residuary legatee, and has even now resulted in making her the owner of Underhill.

"But an hour ago she was attacked with intent to kill. The murderer, who had been about to visit me—we may suppose with a similar intent—had been obliged to give up that attempt because Miss Wing was with me in Hutter's room. The murderer passed straight from my bedroom to Miss Wing's, hid in the closet there, and assaulted her when she came in; afterwards taking the opportunity of a few moments to slip away. A fearful risk; and as I dashed from my room to Miss Wing's I knew why it had been taken. One of us, Miss Wing or myself, must die; and one of us would do. If I died, whatever case I had prepared against Miss Wing would die with me, and if she died that fact exonerated her from responsibility for the other deaths, and nullified my evidence, which could only be circumstantial—since she was innocent.

"And why must Miss Wing be exonerated at all costs? Because if she were to be convicted of the crime of murdering Florence Mason, she could not inherit under Florence Mason's will."

Gamadge paused, and let his eyes rest on the intent faces before him. Mason's was dreadfully pale, Mrs. Deedes's drawn and frightened, Susie Burt's a terrified mask spotted with make-up. Corinne Hutter, her bit of sewing in her hands, leaned forward, frankly absorbed; Percy alone showed no interest. He was thinking of other things, or seemed to be. Gamadge went on:

"Underhill. It runs through this case, an ever-recurrent name, constant as the rush of its stream. I knew that its inclusion in Miss Wing's legacy must have significance, but why was it left her? It has no youthful associations for her; and I should think few happy ones. Her future interests do not lie here. Why should she be expected to strain her resources—strain them increasingly, I suppose, as time goes on—to maintain this isolated house and property? Mrs. Mason told me she wanted it; others, I found, wanted it more.

"It had become evident to me from my first talk with Florence Mason, and later from the remarks of others, that Florence had a secret counsellor; one with great influence, greater influence than any servant could have, one whom Florence trusted as she trusted no one else among her friends. That person had already convinced Florence that Miss Wing had not tampered with the novel; was it possible that that person had forced Underhill into Miss Wing's legacy? And had that person actually preferred to kill Miss Wing rather than lose the chance of acquiring Underhill through her?

"But how, I asked myself, could the murderer acquire Underhill if Evelyn Wing were dead? Mrs. Deedes is her cousin's natural heir, and there is no reason to suppose that she would hand Underhill over to anyone else. I could only imagine some agreement between Evelyn Wing and the unknown. Miss Wing may in all innocence have mortgaged her future to this supposed friend, or may have made a will in the friend's favour. At any rate, I was sure that it must be someone whom she would never suspect of murder, and who had, or pretended to have, a heavy claim upon her."

Mason spoke hoarsely. "Underhill in itself doesn't mean a thing to me. I only want a farm—a place to breed horses and

make a living. You're all wrong, Gamadge; it was the money—
the money. Hutter was killed too."

"Hutter was killed too." Gamadge turned his head to look
out at rolling hemlock forest and a clearing, wintry sky. "Hutter
was killed so that Mrs. Mason's residuary legatee should have
millions; millions beside which Underhill and its upkeep
would seem a trifle to be given away to a deserving applicant.
The Hutters acquired this land a century ago, cleared it,
farmed it, built and rebuilt the house. A Hutter left the place
and made money; there was a feud, how deep, how mortal, we
don't know; but Nahum's daughter lived here in wealth, and
Joel's only child sat day by day in the village library in
Erasmus, and refused an annuity of five hundred dollars a
year." He turned his head to look at Corinne Hutter. "You had
time for brooding, Miss Hutter," he said; "but it is not well to
brood."

"What are you talking about?" Astonished, she half rose;
her narrow chin drew back, her large and high forehead under
its line of black hair dominated all her features but the bright
round eyes.

"About your obsession—Underhill."

"You mean I killed my cousin to get this place? You mean I
thought I could get it from Evelyn Wing? It doesn't make sense."

"I have offered a theory."

"You must have gone right out of your head."

"Sit down and let me tell you how I worked up to it."

She gave him the oddest, quizzical look, and sank slowly
down on the settee. "I guess you could talk yourself into almost
anything," she said, "but what's the use of it? Nobody will believe
you."

"Let me try to make them believe me. I must begin by saying that from the very first, subtle and cautious as you were, you
betrayed yourself in one respect—you wouldn't allow a breath of
suspicion to fall on Evelyn Wing. Of all the people in this house

I could say then, and I say now, that you alone were definitely shielding someone—*at the expense of others.*"

She seemed about to speak, but thought better of it; gave him that curious, inquiring look, and was silent.

"You were about to say something?" he asked.

"I was about to say that I never heard such nonsense. If I wanted Underhill I could have asked Cousin Florence to leave it to me. I refused."

"You refused five hundred a year. Mrs. Mason would never have left you Underhill; never in the world. And even if she had been willing to leave it to you, would you have cared to wait for it until you were perhaps twenty-five years older? Florence might have had a long life. And now we come to the second paradox in the case, and its greatest irony; by disinheriting you, Florence created the only human being she could trust."

For the first time Percy moved; he turned his head to look at Gamadge, who responded to the look by repeating his words in emphasis:

"The only one she could trust. She loved many, but she could only put faith in the one who had nothing to gain from her, during her life and after her death. That's what Nahum Hutter taught his children to believe of human nature; I've heard him doing it, and my flesh crept."

"I wouldn't have his money," said Corinne.

"You would have it, but not a mere insulting crumb of it, tossed to you by his children. A long time ago you began to work out schemes for acquiring Underhill; a long time ago you dreamed of tearing up every brick in that formal garden. At last you found a way, since you had found a person whom you could practise upon. You began the campaign by tampering with Florence Mason's script."

"I wasn't even in the house!"

"You undoubtedly had keys to it, after all the years you had worked here; and you have a car. You know books, you are familiar with the typewriter; and with what pleasure, what rapture, you must have studied Percy's choice of reading matter, and settled upon those quotations!"

She slowly turned her head and looked over her shoulder. "Mr. Macloud."

He responded instantly. "Right here, Corinne."

"This isn't evidence?"

"Not a word of it."

"Then must I listen to it?"

"Hear him out. Perhaps he'll do better."

"I'll do better," said Gamadge. "Having accepted as true Miss Wing's story that she had seen Percy, or thought she had seen him, in the garden, I asked myself whom she could have seen; since I also accepted as true his denial of having been there. Not Mason, who is blond; not Mrs. Deedes, whose hair is grey; not the auburn Miss Burt, whose hair could probably not have been seen over the hedge at all. If she saw dark hair under a hat, I could only suppose that she had seen yours.

"Well; there I was, and there I remained. I was forced to tempt you into betraying yourself by a trick that failed; but even while it failed—and here we arrive at the third paradox in the case—it gave me the evidence I needed; and even as I saw that evidence, and acted on it to save Evelyn Wing's life, I remembered in a flash the single abnormality in your conduct, in anybody's conduct since the case opened. Why I asked myself, as I fled down the hall, should you have brought your sewing kit to Underhill?"

Her eyes rested on his unwaveringly; but her attitude had changed. Her back, straight as ever, looked rigid.

"Why on earth," continued Gamadge, "should you have arranged to do sewing here, on your holiday, when all you said you had planned was to walk and sleep? And why should a curtain in Underhill have a rent in it? I have not asked those superparlourmaids whether that curtain—in a guest room, you know, even though it is a small guest room—*had* a rent in it; but I don't think it had. Louise would have brought it to their attention, if their trained eyes had missed it."

She leaned back in her chair, hands deep in her pockets, legs outstretched in front of her, feet crossed; never had Gamadge seen her make herself comfortable before, and he at least knew that she had relaxed because the battle, for her, was over.

"But conclusive as that evidence must be," he said, "I have evidence as good, evidence of which you know nothing. You have not looked, Miss Hutter, at the soles of your shoes."

With a movement indescribably furtive she placed one foot on the other knee, and looked at it. Then she looked up at him.

"You no doubt observe," said Gamadge, "the silvery film that is ground into the leather, and that won't come off without intensive scrubbing. It's powder, the sticky kind that won't come out of carpet unless you go at it hard. The griffons spilled Macloud's talcum on the tiles of that bathroom; and when I went to unfasten the door you had bolted I saw your footprints on my rug. They are fainter in the hall, still fainter in Miss Wing's room; but they are there. And nobody has been in my room or bath since, and two officers are now guarding the hall."

In obedience to Windorp's shouted order, Morse had fled; Gamadge heard him talking to Beaver, and then heard him telephoning in the library. But Windorp was demanding an answer to another question:

"What's that about sewing up a tear in a curtain?"

"Oh; you'll want witnesses when you look in her sewing kit. I should say there's an extra capsule—one of the red capsules, you know—in the middle of a spool of cotton. White cotton. It would just fit. But I think—look out; look out for that thimble."

She had withdrawn a hand from her sweater pocket; her brass thimble was on her finger, and Windorp, snatching it off, removed from inside it a spiral of tissue paper. He sniffed it, and his face was a study as he gazed at her.

"That thimble is too big for me," she told him. "Your policewoman didn't bother with it; she didn't hardly interrupt my sewing."

"I don't think you'll see a policewoman again, Miss Hutter," said Gamadge. "You'll see a nurse and doctors. You are a madwoman."

"Am I?" She returned his grave look with one as profound.

"You are, and I only hope that that agreement—whatever it is—won't make it look like premeditated murder for money. If it weren't for that agreement, you know, people would think of you sitting there in Erasmus, day after day, and your rich relations up here at Underhill. They'd remember what Nahum Hutter was like, and they'd remember the old family feud, and they'd say no wonder you lost your wits. I don't think you'd ever see the inside of a court-house, and you'd end your days comfortably enough in an asylum; criminally insane. But an agreement looks like conspiracy; and madness doesn't conspire—not your kind of madness. It plays a lone hand."

She was watching him intently. After a pause she said: "I guess you're right. I didn't have any agreement with Evelyn Wing; just a verbal understanding that she'd let me have part of her income because I got her the job. I knew she'd let me have Underhill."

Mrs. Deedes, as if bewitched, sat looking dumbly at her. Macloud looked at Gamadge as if he had just seen him produce a globe of goldfish from a top hat. Windorp asked: "You think Evelyn Wing would have given you this place—without any signed agreement—just because you got her the job with Mrs. Mason?"

"I know she would have."

"Then you *are* crazy."

"Yes; didn't Mr Gamadge say I am?"

CHAPTER TWENTY

Case History

*E*ARLY DUSK WAS FALLING WHEN Gamadge walked into Mrs. Deedes's room. It was littered with tissue paper, bags and cases, and she sat among her possessions with her grey dress across her knees.

"Well, Sally." He shook his head at her. "You've been very wicked."

The grey dress slid to the floor. "Oh, Henry," she wailed, "how did you know?"

"You were in such a confounded dither from the first; and Corinne Hutter was protecting you, too, though I didn't see fit to mention it."

"I nearly fainted when you began to talk about her protecting Evelyn. I sat there and wondered whether you were really going to keep me out of it; I didn't see how you could."

"Let's hope Windorp didn't see you nearly faint."

"Won't Corinne tell?"

"Certainly not. The last thing she wants is to have the conspiracy element brought forward."

"I never dreamed of conspiracy!"

"It looks like conspiracy; in fact, it was conspiracy."

"Bill would never forgive me! He'd never marry me over again!" Mrs. Deedes hunted about among the litter on the bed, and snatched up a handkerchief. She wiped streaming tears from her cheeks. Gamadge, propped against a carved bedpost, hands in pockets and head lowered, watched her with a kind of grudging sympathy.

"I must confess," he said, "that I was thinking of Bill when I reprehensibly saved you at the expense of your cousin Miss Evelyn Wing. Bill has his faults, but they're out in the open. He wouldn't have cared for this."

"Oh, Henry, are you sure about Corinne?"

"My dear child, Corinne took my broad hint and will act upon it. She will be declared insane before the case ever gets before the grand jury. And unless I'm very much mistaken she will *be* insane within a few years. Schizophrenia, paranoia, dementia praecox—I don't know what they call it; but she's well on the way to it now."

Mrs. Deedes, her tears wiped away, gazed plaintively up at him. "She always seemed so sensible!"

"She has a ratlike cunning. I dare say she began life as the most intelligent of all the Hutters; but there was something wrong. I knew there was something wrong when I was confronted with the greatest of all the paradoxes in the case—the paradox of her having refused a Hutter legacy, while yet remaining on good terms with the Hutters. That called for an abnormality of cleverness, or else a kind of otherworldliness that I was quite sure she didn't have. Percy saw that she didn't have it, and vaguely diagnosed madness to come; but of course he wasn't interested in Corinne Hutter."

"She must be absolutely mad now, to have run those risks."

"Except for that last flurry when she risked getting out of Evelyn Wing's room and around the corner into the back passage before anybody appeared in the hall, she had too much opportunity for watching chances to run much risk of any kind. And even then, even in those seconds after Evelyn Wing had been shut into the closet, she knew where the patrol was and knew that I must be on my way to unbolt the bathroom door."

"Oh dear, I thought she had so much character!"

"She had. You'd better tell me all about the conspiracy, Sally. I don't think you can be quite out of the woods yet."

"It all happened so naturally, it was just like the simplest business transaction. Florence met Evelyn at my apartment, and liked her looks and her game of bridge and everything, and was so much interested in her story and the hard time she'd been having. She told Corinne about her, and one day Corinne arrived in New York and asked to meet Evelyn herself. She said she'd just come to town to see the exhibition of Italian old masters at the Museum of Modern Art."

"I wonder whether she saw and admired Parmigiano's 'Portrait of a Lady'—subject unknown. It suddenly occurs to me as an excellent portrait of Corinne Hutter."

"Henry you must be out of your senses. Corinne like that? It's a portrait of somebody of the Renaissance nobility!"

"Put Corinne in robes and jewels, do up her hair—why, even the pose is the same! That characteristic leaning a little forward, looking straight at you. Some think Parmigiano's lady is beautiful, some think she looks like a rat; both schools are right, and I only wish I had thought of it when I first saw her looking down at me from the back stairs. 'Now that,' I said to myself, 'is a personality.'"

"Well, I never thought of her as a personality, but I knew she always had lots of influence with Florence."

"Oh, Sally, Sally."

"I know, Henry, but how could I dream she was capable of

murder? I thought it was Tim Mason and that horrid little Susie
Burt. Well, Corinne met Evelyn, and was sure she'd do beauti-
fully as Florence's secretary and I told her about lending Evelyn
a thousand dollars to take a business course, and live on while she
was taking it. I couldn't afford to lend it to her, but she was penniless, and had been ill, and jobs aren't easy to get. Bill made me."

"And Miss Hutter suggested that you ought to protect the
loan?"

"Yes, because I had no security I thought her idea about the
agreement was so clever; it was with Evelyn, you know. Corinne
told me how to draw it up; it gave me half Evelyn's income for
five years."

Gamadge closed his eyes. "Income, not salary," he murmured. Then, looking at Mrs. Deedes with a certain incredulity
he asked: "Were you expecting about a hundred and fifty percent
on your money?"

"No, of course not. Just the regular thing, six percent, like
any loan. And when I had got the thousand dollars and the interest back, I simply banked the rest; saved it for her, you know,
and sent her an accounting. In case she was out of work again,
you know, or ill, or something. One really couldn't count on poor
Florrie."

"Five years—just enough time to get Florence well pinned
down. Miss Wing came here four years ago. You've been had,
Sally."

"How could I know? At the time it seemed only fair, and
Evelyn was glad to sign. She hates being under an obligation."

"She was created, in fact, to serve the purposes of Miss
Corinne Hutter."

"Well, I didn't intend to cheat her! We had a notary witness
our signatures, and of course I never dreamed that Evelyn would
ever have anything but a few years of salary. Then Corinne came
in one day, about six months later, and said that Florence liked
her so much that she might actually adopt her, and was sure to

leave her something in her will; unless something happened, of course. Corinne explained that Tim Mason was getting nervous about Florence's interest in Evelyn, and that Florence, being fickle and easily swayed, needed a lot of handling. Corinne said perhaps I'd like to make another agreement this time with her; to go half and half with her on my share of Evelyn's income from then on while Evelyn kept the job.

"I knew very well that Evelyn wouldn't keep the job if Corinne made trouble for her. So I—"

"Submitted to extortion."

"Well, it was value received; Corinne took a good deal of trouble with it. But she said she'd like to have something else in our agreement, too; she said that if Florence should die, leaving Evelyn something considerable in her will, something equivalent to the value of Underhill plus Underhill itself, say, Corinne would waive all other claims on my share of Evelyn's income in favour of Underhill and enough cash to pay the taxes."

"Great heavens."

"Well, Henry, what could I do? I didn't expect Florence to die in five years, or to leave Underhill to Evelyn Wing! I thought it was just pride on Corinne's part, a sort of forlorn hope. Because as she explained to me, she couldn't take anything directly from the Hutters on account of a dying promise she made her father."

"She took something directly from the Hutters, all right. I only hope this never gets before a judge and a jury—you'd have to plead insanity yourself."

"It didn't sound insane, the way she put it; she said she'd like to run Underhill as a boarding-house or summer resort, and of course the taxes aren't much up here. And she could have done it, too."

"When Sylvanus and Florence were killed, and you found out that Underhill had been left to Miss Wing, all as per schedule, weren't you sharply reminded of that agreement?"

"I was frightened and worried, of course; but Corinne told me Tim and Susie had done it, she had proof, but she wouldn't say what it was on Florence's account."

"No wonder you put it on the spirits! Did Corinne Hutter think Miss Wing was going to stick to that agreement with you, and that you would stick to yours with her, when the basis of the transaction rose from a few hundreds a year to a good many thousands?"

"Evelyn would have been glad to stick to hers with me, and I had to stick to mine with Corinne!"

"And how was Miss Wing to be persuaded to turn Underhill over to you, and what would she have thought when you turned it over to Miss Corinne Hutter?"

"It would have seemed natural enough to her—Corinne is a Hutter, and Evelyn feels very grateful to me, and is fond of Bill."

"Where the devil are these precious agreements, Sally? Will the police find them?"

"Oh, no. Mine with Evelyn is here in my bag, and Corinne's is in a book in the Erasmus library."

"And why shouldn't somebody take the book out, since Miss Hutter isn't there to sit on it?"

"Oh, nobody would take it out. It's the *Proceedings of the Erasmus Bible and Foreign Mission Society* for 1910; they had a pageant, and took pictures, and Sylvanus had it bound up for them."

"Nothing even distantly allied to regional Americana is safe from research in these days. You must get the book out to-morrow."

"I meant to get it this afternoon."

"And now give me that thing you made your cousin sign in her hour of need."

She fumbled in her bag and got out a paper. He looked at it in disgust, burned it over an ash-tray, and dropped the last charred corner into the fireplace. "There," he said. "That's all I can do. If Evelyn Wing should get into trouble about this, you know, you will have to face the music."

"Of course I shall."

"If you refuse, I'll have to talk to Bill."

He left her, still shaking his head, and went along the hall to Evelyn Wing's room. She was sitting up in bed, pale but smiling, and the high white bandage around her neck made her look like a young gentleman of the Regency. Percy, established on the bed's edge, contemplated her fondly.

"Don't get up." Gamadge pressed his shoulder, and moved past him to draw up a chair.

"Mr. Gamadge"—she put out her hand—"I'm so grateful."

"I don't know why you should be; it was only by accident that I saw Corinne Hutter's footprints on my rug; and your friend here will tell you that I brought your name into the discourse with which I tried to convince Miss Hutter that she must plead insane."

"I thought of that agreement that I signed with Sally; but I never signed any with Corinne Hutter."

"Of course not, and you can swear you didn't, and Corinne Hutter will swear you didn't. I think the authorities will decide that the whole thing was a figment of her imagination, and the murders committed from pure spite. I hoped you might be willing to assist in the rescue of poor Sally, who after all wasn't grafting for herself."

"They won't ask me about the agreement with Sally?"

"Not a word. No such agreement now exists."

"Sally was always saying that if we ever had money we must do something for Corinne, and that it would be so nice to keep Underhill in the Hutter family. When I knew that Mrs. Mason had left it to me in her will I began to be awfully worried about Sally, and at last I was afraid she had actually killed Mrs. Mason and Mr. Hutter, and might be going to kill you."

"So you came in to assist with planchette, and watch the door. I was annoyed, I can tell you."

"When I felt that leash around my neck I knew it couldn't be Sally. I knew it!"

"And then you knew no more."

Percy snatched her hand from Gamadge's, and clasped it, with her other one, between his own. "Let's just quietly expunge the incident from our tablets of memory," he said. "Let's forget the whole thing. For two days I've been going around in a kind of mental strait jacket, afraid to show feeling because I thought I would be supposed to be covering up for my friend here; and all the time I was sure Mason had done it, with Susie scouting for him, and that he'd never be found out and Evelyn would take the rap. When did Corinne get that leash off its hook in the servants' sitting-room?"

"Two minutes after she put it there, I suppose," said Gamadge. "As soon as the coast was clear."

"I suppose she used to drive over when we were in New York and go through the house and all our things," said Evelyn Wing. "I suppose she found my blue slacks in the box in my closet. I did say something about them to Cousin Sally."

Percy, looking at her through half-closed eyes, said: "You've got square with your Cousin Sally now. Curse that thousand dollars!"

"I don't know what would have become of me if she hadn't lent me the money to take that business course. Mr. Gamadge, you don't know what it's like to have nothing, absolutely nothing. It's easy to say you'd rather starve than do things, but I wanted to pay Sally back, and I was fond of Mrs. Mason, and I had to live."

"So you solemnly typed at her novel, and let her think it would get by. Perhaps it would have got by," said Gamadge. "I don't know."

"I did worse than that, I—"

"Let her abuse you when she felt cross at somebody else.

We know," said Percy. "We knew Mrs. Mason. I don't know why Corinne went on with her scheme after you got into the house, though," he added, turning his dark glance on Gamadge. "I don't think I should have risked it myself."

"I never seemed very formidable to Corinne Hutter," replied Gamadge, "and you must remember that she was pressed for time. You and Miss Wing might have decided to run off and get married, the Masons might have made up their differences, and Florence might have drafted another will. What on earth were you two bickering about, anyway?"

"Difficult question," said Percy, "but I think you might as well know all the answers. First: when I met Evelyn, and recognized her as my fate, Susie Burt had just lost the remains of her parents' money. It wasn't the moment to break with her."

"But wasn't she breaking with you? She seemed to me sincerely preoccupied with Mason."

"The trouble is, so few people seem to understand Susie's type. People like Susie don't fall in love much, and even when they do, they want to keep all their men around them still. Susie Burt cannot, absolutely cannot, give up a man; if she had five hundred men, she'd go through anything to keep the five hundred and first. A couple of weeks ago I told her she cared for Mason, and it was all off with me; I wouldn't play second fiddle to a married guy. She wanted me to string along, and we had an uproar."

"And Corinne Hutter was always telling me," said Evelyn Wing, "that Glen really liked Susie best."

"And she tried to annoy Mr. Mason into turning him out for good," suggested Gamadge, "by telling her that he was annoying you with his attentions."

"I'll annoy you with my attentions from now on." Percy took her face gently between his hands. "Until I get you married to me. Then I'll be off your hands—flying."

She put her arms around his neck. Gamadge quietly retired, and found when he reached his room that his bag was packed and ready. Macloud joined him on the stairs, and the two Danes, calmly insistent, followed them with the luggage.

Macloud said gloomily: "I had to let Susie Burt drive down with us."

"Curses. Is she leaving?"

"Yes, and she looked very glum; I couldn't refuse to give her the lift, but I told her we had weighty matters to discuss, and that she'd have to sit with the bags."

"How about Sally? Isn't she ready to come?"

"She got the invitation Susie didn't get—from Mason. She's staying."

"Staying? She was packing up a quarter of an hour ago."

"Five minutes ago Louise came in to say good-bye, and tell me that she'd been engaged to stay and look after Mrs. Deedes. I'm glad poor old Sally can have a maid again." He gave Gamadge a sidelong look.

"So am I."

"Louise said she always hated Corinne, who had what amounted to powers of life and death over them all; but they were too afraid of her to complain."

Mason awaited them at the foot of the stairs. Macloud took leave of him, and went on out to the car, but he kept hold of Gamadge's arm. "Can't express my gratitude," he mumbled. "I thought—Lord knows what I thought. I was blaming myself." He glanced out at Macloud's Sedan, and Susie Burt's flaming hair against the dark interior.

"Never mind. It's all over now."

"This thing has shaken me, though; I can't help feeling that it was partly my fault. I'm not proud of myself."

Gamadge looked down at the upturned face of the griffons, who sat close together beside Mason's left foot. He said: "Thank these little creatures, not me."

"They're good little devils. Gamadge—Windorp says he

thinks you're right; he thinks Corinne Hutter's crazy. He says he'll never forget the cool way she took it when you sprung the evidence."

"If she's not crazy now, I think she soon will be."

"She was going to take that stuff she was carrying around in that thimble—wasn't she?" Mason's face expressed a childlike horror.

"Well, I suppose so. She wouldn't like the idea of sitting through her own trial. But she'll be all right now," said Gamadge. "Now she'll be a mental invalid, and an interesting case. Nothing humiliating about that."

"Damn; when I think of Florence and Syl—"

"*She* thought of them. Thought of them too long."

Mrs. Deedes rushed down the stairs and threw herself into his arms. "Henry, darling Henry, Bill's coming! Evelyn doesn't want Underhill, Tim; you can have it for a nominal price, and Bill and I will stay as long as you like."

"Glad of company," said Mason.

"Splendid." Gamadge, released, settled his tie. When he at last got away, and down the front steps of the house, he turned for a last look at Underhill. Its rosy face was in shadow, and there was something mortified and forlorn about the look of it, decked out as it was in the trappings that had been meant to save it from its old pomposity.

"I wouldn't live there now," he told Macloud, getting into the car, "for a good deal."

Macloud started the engine. "It will be lived in, though," he said, "but by people with thicker skins than yours, and shorter memories."

"I should always be remembering how Corinne Hutter wanted it." He looked out of the car window at frowning slopes of hemlock. "Sally had better be careful; sometimes she may get a glimpse of an astral body on the stairs."